The Tale of

Jessica
Sweetapple

Also by Linda Kempton

The Naming of William Rutherford
Who'll Catch the Nightmares?

For younger readers

Tiny the Terrier

The Tale of Jessica Sweetapple

LINDA KEMPTON

with illustrations by Martin Ursell

mammoth

This story is dedicated to my ancestors, who gave me not only their names but inspiration too. It is dedicated especially to my mother, Kathleen Glew. My thanks to Gill Vickery, who found the name Sweetapple in a Quaker cemetery in Leicester, and to Cally Poplak, who helped me to see the wood as well as the trees.

First published in Great Britain in 2000 by Mammoth,
an imprint of Egmont Children's Books Limited,
a division of Egmont Holding Limited,
239 Kensington High Street, London W8 6SA

ISBN 0 7497 3905 3

10 9 8 7 6 5 4 3 2 1

A CIP catalogue record for this title is available from the British Library

Printed and bound in Great Britain by Cox & Wyman Ltd, Reading, Berkshire

Contents

Miasma

School

Apple Manor

Family Tree

Jessica's room

Moat

To be ignorant of what happened before you were born is to remain a child for ever.
Cicero.

Door to the Ancestors

A great ship plunged through the wall
of Jessica Sweetapple's bedroom.
Not a whole ship; just the front part,
the prow. It was as high as the ceiling
and as wide as the wall. The room was
full of ship. In the daytime it towered
above Jessica Sweetapple's head. But at
night she entered into it to learn the
wisdom of the Ancestors and the
secrets of Grandma Liddell.

Part One

The
Special
Child

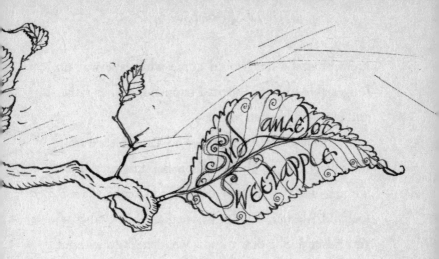

1. The Family Tree

Jessica stepped out of the ship and into her bedroom. The door to the ship was still open and she could hear the slip-slip-slip of the sea and the sighs of the Ancestors. 'Goodbye, Grandma Liddell,' she called. 'Goodbye, Grandpa Liddell, goodbye, Great-Uncle Nelson Sweetapple. I'll be back as soon as I can.'

Jessica shut the door and leaned against it. She hated saying goodbye; she hated leaving the ship. She knew that the day would come when she was no longer able to return. It had happened to her father and it would happen to her.

She thought of her friends who had vanished from the village, ticked them off on her fingers: Oliver, Thomas and Guy, Kathryn, Sally and Coralie, Lauren, Joel and Alastair, Tony and Jonathan, Janet, Michael and Edward. She didn't know what she'd do without the Ancestors now that all her friends were gone. Her friends and her father.

Her thoughts were interrupted by her mother's voice, drifting up from the hall. 'Do you know what time it is, Jessica Sweetapple? You'll be late for school!'

Late? Early? What did it matter? Jessica closed her ears to her mother's voice. What was the point of school when the strange new children never spoke, except in whispers; when the whispers were always about Jessica?

She leaned against the open window of her bedroom and scraped the snow from the window-ledge outside. Snow had settled in the round snail curves of the window latch. It had covered the trees and fields and houses.

'Jessica! Come on down this minute!'

Jessica sighed and wiped the snow from her hand. She took one last look at the ship. She waved to the Ancestors but, of course, they couldn't see her; and they mustn't come out of the ship because the ship was the place where Ancestors belonged. They belonged out on the sea, and deep beneath the swirling ocean.

Down in the big square hallway, Mother lifted Jessica's coat from the Family Tree. The Family Tree grew up through a square patch of soil in the floor, and spread its gnarled and ancient branches into the silent air of the hallway. Great-Uncle Nelson Sweetapple liked to tell Jessica the story of the tree, and she thought about it now as her mother held out her warm winter coat.

Long, long ago, a pip had fallen to the ground, accidentally dropped by Sir Lancelot Sweetapple who was out riding his horse. The pip grew and grew into the Family Tree, and Sir Lancelot built Apple Manor round it. But the bricks of the house shut out the light and the Family Tree drooped and almost died. So Sir Lancelot Sweetapple ordered huge windows to be made to let the light back in. The Family Tree had flourished in the light of Apple Manor from that time onwards. It was meant to be there.

Jessica put out her hand and touched its trunk. Her mother tutted impatiently and shook the coat. 'Jessica!'

In spring the tree was covered in pink blossom. When the blossom fell on to the black and white tiles of the hallway floor, the family would leave it there because it was a promise of fruit and looked so pretty. But now Miss Darknight had come and she sucked it up into the vacuum cleaner. In autumn, the branches were weighed down with large green cooking apples which Mother made into pies and chutneys and crumbles. But when Miss Darknight found them, she threw them on the compost heap at the bottom of the garden to moulder and rot, to wriggle and squirm with maggots.

Now it was winter time, and had been ever since Father left. The branches of the tree were bare; bare except for the Sweetapple leaves. Each time a Sweetapple baby was born, the tree put out a special new leaf in celebration. The veins of the leaf spelled out the name of the infant in curly, spidery gold writing. It also put out leaves for those who had married into the family, like Jessica's mother; but the writing of their names was not so beautiful. The tree liked Sweetapples.

'Hurry up, Jessica,' her mother said. 'Miss Darknight's waiting.'

Jessica shuddered. She wished that Miss Darknight would go away and never come back. She had applied for the job of housekeeper at Apple Manor and now Mother didn't seem able to get rid of her. In fact, Mother didn't seem able to do anything since she'd arrived. It was as though Miss Darknight had stolen something from inside Mrs Sweetapple, so that she was no longer the same, strong, laughing person that she had been. Sometimes it seemed that Miss Darknight made Mrs Sweetapple say things that she couldn't possibly mean. Like now, for instance. Her mother hardly ever used to get cross before.

'Jessica, for goodness sake! What are you doing?'

'Sorry.' She sighed and slipped her arms into the sleeves of her coat.

'As I was saying, Miss Darknight will take you to school today. I always lose my feet in the snow.'

Jessica looked down at her mother's feet. Both of them there. Neither missing.

'You must always find them again, then,' she said.

'Not always,' said Mrs Sweetapple with a sigh.

Miss Darknight held out her stiff white fingers. 'Come!' she ordered. Her voice was sharp, tense, like a small dog's yaps.

Jessica looked up. Miss Darknight seemed almost as tall as the Family Tree, yet no one ever saw her come or go. She was either there, or not there.

She took the woman's hand. But as soon as their fingers touched she wanted to pull away. Miss Darknight's fingers were as cold as the white marble headstones in the churchyard. They were all bone. Cold, white bone. Cold as Christmas without any presents.

Miss Darknight strode across the hall like a tall black stick, pulling Jessica with her as she hauled open the big oak door that led into the garden.

'Goodbye, darling,' Mother called.

Jessica turned to wave but already her mother was beginning to fade against the trunk of the Family Tree.

'Goodbye, Jessica Sweetapple,' whispered the old house as she stepped into the snow. 'Goodbye.'

'Goodbye, house. Goodbye, Ancestors,' Jessica replied.

'There are no Ancestors!' Miss Darknight snapped. 'I've told you before.'

'Yes there are! There's Grandma and Grandpa Liddell, and Great-Uncle Nelson Sweetapple and Solomon Sweetapple and . . .'

'Fiddlesticks! Dreams and imagination and fiddlesticks!'

'Grandma Liddell's not imagination, she's real! She

tells me stories of Ithaca, Odysseus, and things beneath the sea. She understands the wisdom of the seahorses!'

'Poppycock!' declared Miss Darknight. 'Poppycock!'

Jessica was close to tears. Miss Darknight was a thief! Not of things, but of dreams and ideas and everything that makes a person real. She crushed them with her bony fingers, sucked them up into her vacuum cleaner, hurled them into dark, maggotty corners.

Why did she stay when she hated them all so much? Why didn't she just go away?

2. School of the wooden children

The snow came halfway up Jessica's boots and covered everything in sight: the pond, the hedge, the garden; perhaps the whole world. She felt like a figure on top of a Christmas cake.

Far along the lane that led to school, she found footprints. They were small footprints, like her own. 'Look, Miss Darknight! Look!' she shouted. 'Children! Let's hurry up and find them. It might be Oliver and Thomas! Or Kathryn! Or Guy!'

'No!' Miss Darknight's face had turned whiter than the snow at her feet. 'There are no children!'

'Yes there are. Look! Can't you see their footprints?' Jessica's heart thudded. If she walked a little faster she would catch up with them. Could it be that her friends were back? Maybe these were Lauren's footprints, or Alastair's or Jonathan's.

'Listen!' She stood as still as the snow on the village rooftops. Somewhere, not far away, children sang.

> *My mother said*
> *I never should*
> *Play with the gypsies*
> *In the wood.*

But Miss Darknight had gone. She had disappeared into thin air, like a ghost, like all of Jessica's friends who had disappeared when the housekeeper came to the village.

The children's voices travelled across the snowy field from the schoolhouse, but it was too far away to tell if these were her friends' voices or not. Jessica skipped on, more and more excited as she neared the school.

She skipped into the schoolroom. The smile on her face froze like the snow in the lanes outside. Her friends hadn't returned. For a moment, Jessica felt as if they'd never really existed, that they were people from a dream she'd had once.

Wooden children sat at her friends' desks. They'd arrived the day after Miss Darknight. Now they stared straight ahead at the wooden teacher. The air in the schoolroom was still as a dead man's breath. Only Jessica breathed. Only Jessica caused the air to stir.

She walked up and down past the rows of desks. She heard the children whispering her name, but when she turned to look at them, their painted mouths were still.

'Jessica Sweetapple!' The voice made her jump. It roared like a bellowing bull. She turned to the teacher whose painted eyes stared out of the window at the snow which had begun to fall again.

'Yes, Miss.' Her voice was small and timid. A mouse, not a bull.

A great wave of laughter flowed through the

schoolroom and when she turned to look at them, the wooden children had moved. Heads, hands, arms, shoulders — all were thrown out at strange wooden angles, as though they were players in a game of statues. One girl's mouth had grown into a jagged red line that ripped across her wooden face.

'Jessica Sweetapple!'

'Yes, Miss.' She looked desperately around her. Then she saw what she was supposed to see. A pin-board glowed with shining red letters. She walked towards it. The letters darted across the pin-board, looking for other letters to team up with. As they slowed and settled, she saw that they had found the places where they belonged. They pulsated with the pleasure of making words.

JESSICA SWEETAPPLE MUST
LEARN TO BE A MORE
FRIENDLY GIRL. SHE WILL
STAY IN AT PLAYTIME UNTIL
HER MANNERS IMPROVE.

The schoolroom filled with laughter and echoes of laughter, until Jessica thought that her head would burst. She covered her ears with her hands and stamped her foot. 'No! No! No!'

'No?' the voices whispered. 'No?'

'No,' said Jessica firmly. 'You're being illogical. How can I learn to be a more friendly girl if I can't go out to play with the others? I need some children to practise on. I want my friends. I want my old teacher back!'

The letters on the pin-board glowed even brighter.

'Illogical, is it?' she heard them whisper.

And then the booming voice came again. Question after question after question:

'What is the capital of France?'

'What is seventy-four divided by thirteen?'

'Who is the President of the United States of America?'

'When was the Battle of Hastings?'

'Where is your essay?'

'Essay?' murmured Jessica.

'Look at what the others have done. Look at these fine examples of schoolwork.'

Jessica looked. She walked up and down the rows of desks again. Wooden pens were clamped in wooden fingers. But no ink flowed. The exercise books were empty. She sat down at her own desk, next to a boy with black painted hair, shiny as melted tar.

'What's the title?' she whispered, as she picked up her pen.

'The title is,' boomed Bellowing Bull, 'Her Gracious Majesty, Queen Elizabeth the Second.'

Jessica picked up her pen and began to write.

> *During the time of Her Gracious Majesty Queen Elizabeth the First, the Family Tree at Apple Manor was attacked by a dark knight. The Sweetapple Family would all have been killed if it had not been for the courage of a Special Child, who had great wisdom . . .*

'What's this?' The disembodied voice boomed round the schoolroom like a gong. 'You were instructed to write about Queen Elizabeth the *Second*, not the *First*. You and your arrogant Sweetapple pride. Special Child indeed! The only special thing about the children in your family is their stupidity. Go and stand in the corner.'

The wooden laughter came in a great wave, like a flood through Jessica's body. No one moved, then Jessica, her face burning with shame, went to stand in the corner. She knew that all the wooden eyes were turned towards her. She wished that the Special Child would come and rescue her.

At playtime Jessica followed the others outside, completely forgetting that she was supposed to stay in. But when she reached the big double doors, a sudden flurry of snow blew into her face. She heard the wild roar of wind. A trickle of ice melted on to the back of her neck. Jessica shook her head and rubbed it away with her scarf. When she looked up again, a sheet of ice had filled the doorway. Through its transparent thickness a dark shadow moved. It beckoned to her with bony fingers. Miss Darknight. What was she doing there? Why was she spying on her?

Jessica stepped backwards. Again the shadow

beckoned. She could see its mouth moving but she couldn't hear anything. She turned and went back into the warmth of the schoolroom where she hugged herself inside her coat, and shivered. She could hear Miss Darknight banging on the sheet of ice which covered the door.

If only the Special Child would come and bring her father back home.

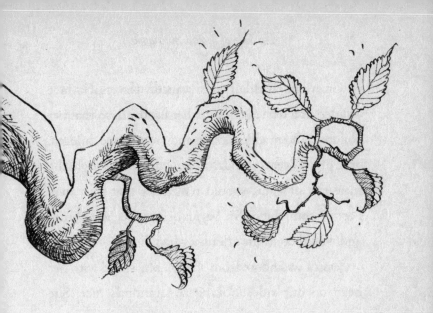

3. A letter from Grandma Liddell

The face of the grandfather clock was the face of Grandpa Liddell. At a quarter to three, the fingers of the clock brushed Grandpa's ears. At twenty to five they skimmed the corners of his mouth. At six o'clock they pointed to the top of his shiny bald head, and the tip of his pointed white beard. The fingers of the clock were joined together at the centre of the clock face, bang in the middle of Grandpa's nose.

Grandma Liddell had wanted the clock face painted as a true likeness of her husband, so that her children, and grandchildren, and great-grandchildren, and great-great-grandchildren, down through the measures of time, should remember that they were part of something that began before they were born, and would continue after they had died.

Jessica was home from school. She stood with her head on one side, looking at Grandpa's face. She smiled. It was the time she liked best, the time when the big finger of the clock reached the top of Grandpa Liddell's bald shiny head, and the little finger touched the edge of his jaw, just below his left ear. Four o'clock. She could go to see Grandma Liddell and the Ancestors, just as she did every day at this time.

She gave a big sigh of relief. Her feet tapped across the black and white tiles of the hallway and up the carved wooden staircase.

'Jessica!'

She stood still. She longed to run away, up to her bedroom and into the ship. But she didn't.

Her mother and Miss Darknight stood side by side in the hall.

'Miss Darknight tells me you've been letting your imagination run away with you again.' Mrs Sweetapple's voice was as gentle as the cooing of doves in the dovecote.

'What does she know?' Jessica stamped her foot angrily. 'Just because she's never seen Grandma Liddell and the others.'

Miss Darknight sniffed: a long, bony sniff that travelled all the way up her long, bony nose.

'Grown-ups know best, Jessica,' her mother said.

But her mother *knew* she wasn't lying! She *knew* about the Ancestors. 'Why are you pretending to be on her side?'

'Listen to what your mother says!' snapped Miss Darknight.

Jessica wanted to scream! She wanted to shout! She wanted to cry! Instead she ran down the stairs and skipped round the Family Tree, chanting:

'*My mother said — I never should — play with the gypsies — in the wood. If I did — she would say — naughty girl to dis-o-bey.*'

The leaves danced in time with her steps. She wouldn't let them see how she felt, how let down by her mother's betrayal.

She saw Miss Darknight finger the brooch on her blouse. It was tarnished and covered in cobwebs. She watched as the housekeeper tried to brush the cobwebs away. But no matter how hard she tried, the cobwebs stayed just where they were.

Mrs Sweetapple caught hold of her daughter, then ran her fingers gently through Jessica's long hair. She bent and kissed the top of her head. 'You'll feel a lot better when Daddy comes back,' she said.

'*If* he ever comes back,' said Miss Darknight.

'Of course he'll come back! He loves us!'

When Miss Darknight came, everything had changed. First the ship's figurehead began to decay. It was supposed to be a wonderful likeness of Sir Lancelot's wife, Lady Imogen, holding a glistening, golden apple. While ever it was there, guarding the ship, Apple Manor and the Sweetapples would be safe.

Then Father had gone away. 'I must go, Jessie,' he'd

said, taking her on to his knee and holding her tight. 'Sir Lancelot came to me in a dream and told me that if I don't find the right piece of wood to carve a new figurehead, then Apple Manor will die. The Ancestors will be cast adrift.'

Already he had travelled halfway round the world, but still he hadn't found it and now there wasn't much time. The figurehead had broken completely away from the ship, and the wound where it had been grew deeper each day and wept sap from its heart. The Ancestors murmured that the time of the Special Child had come.

'You'll feel a lot better when Daddy comes back,' said Mother once more. 'Won't you, darling?'

'He's not coming back,' Miss Darknight whispered.

Jessica turned away because she couldn't bear to look at the woman any more and, as she did so, she saw that a leaf was shaking on the Family Tree. There was a blur of yellow as it shook faster and faster. She knew immediately what it was. 'Look!' she called. 'Grandma's left a message for me.'

She reached far up to the tree's tall branches. A

yellow envelope hung from Grandma Liddell's leaf. It was shaped like Grandma Liddell's face and had her features painted on it. Across the middle of the envelope, right across Grandma's nose, were written the words: *For Jessica Sweetapple.*

But just as she was about to take the letter, a long, bony arm brushed her aside. Fingers, straight and stiff as pencils, pulled the envelope from the tree.

'Give it to me! It's mine!'

'Silly girl. What nonsense is this?' Miss Darknight waved the letter in the air, out of Jessica's reach. Then, with both hands, she lifted it high above her head and slowly began to tear it.

Jessica pushed Miss Darknight right in her bony middle. The woman folded like a deckchair and collapsed on to the floor. Before she had time to recover, Jessica swooped on top of her and tugged the envelope from her hands. She was rewarded by the sight of one of Grandma Liddell's big brown eyes closing across the envelope in an enormous wink. The old woman liked to play jokes.

Jessica scrambled to her feet and darted away from

the housekeeper's clutches. But there was no need: Miss Darknight had gone. She looked around in case the woman was hiding somewhere, waiting to pounce. But no, there was only her mother, hands pressed against her mouth as if she were stifling a scream.

Jessica tore open the envelope carefully, so as not to inflict any more damage on her grandmother's face. The letter said:

> *Where are you, Jessica? I've been waiting for you for ages. Surely you're back from school by now? Hurry up and come. Time is growing short.*
> *With love from Grandma Liddell*

'See, Mother?' Jessica showed her mother the letter. 'This isn't my imagination, is it?'

Mrs Sweetapple smiled weakly, as if she couldn't make up her mind whether it was or it wasn't.

Anger burned in Jessica's heart. Mother had always understood about the Ancestors; it was one of the reasons Father had married her. It was all Miss

Darknight's fault; she'd convinced Mother that the Ancestors weren't real. Now she wouldn't even believe Grandma's letter.

'Do you think I wrote it myself? Do you think I made it all up? Mother you *know* this letter's from Grandma. Look at it!' She sighed with frustration; her mother didn't seem to have enough strength to take the letter from her outstretched hand.

'Oh, Jessica,' sighed Mrs Sweetapple again. 'I don't seem to know what's happening at Apple Manor any more. What are we going to do?'

'We've got to get rid of Miss Darknight. Look what she's doing to you. She's evil. She's got to go!'

'Jess, even if I had the energy, I wouldn't know where to begin.'

'Shut her out of the house.'

But how do you shut someone out of the house when they're able to appear and disappear out of nowhere?

Jessica turned and ran across the marble hall once more; she needed to see the Ancestors. Up the dark wooden staircase she ran, along the gallery, past the family portraits and suits of armour, into her own room and towards the door of the ship.

Across the door, in bold, curly letters, was carved the name, Nelson Sweetapple. Nelson Sweetapple was Jessica's great-great-great – she didn't know how many greats – uncle, long-ago sailor and builder of ships. His emblem had been the seahorse, and every ship he'd built had carried the seal of a hidden seahorse. This one was on the door, beneath his name, and now Jessica pushed and turned it until she heard a click. She stepped through the door of the great wooden ship, and closed it carefully behind her. Then she gave a big sigh. It was a relief to escape the terrible atmosphere in the house.

4. Standing in the sky

*E*verything was dark. Jessica closed her eyes and listened. She could hear the shush, shush, shush of the sea. She could hear the swish of dolphins' tails and the sweet singing of mermaids. Something creaked, creaked, creaked.

In the dark she felt for the second door; the door with the warm handle. Her hand closed round it and its warmth travelled up her arm, along her shoulder and right through her body. When she was filled with the warmth of the ship she pulled the door open. Immediately a strong sea breeze tugged at her hair and her clothing. She saw overhead a deep blue sky and white clouds scudding across it. The breeze was filled with the sharp, salt tang of the sea. She licked the taste of it from her lips.

As she stepped out on to the wooden boards of the deck, she could feel the gentle rocking of the ship. The masts and rigging of a great galleon soared above her head, so high that they seemed to disappear into the sky.

'Jessica!'

She looked around her. The voice came from far away.

'Who is it?' she called.

'Great-Uncle Nelson. Up here.'

She looked up once more. Her eyes travelled up as far as the sky. And there, standing in the sky itself, was Great-Uncle Nelson Sweetapple. When she looked more carefully, she saw that he wasn't really standing in the sky at all. He was standing in the crow's nest, a wooden platform, right at the top of the rigging.

'Come on up!' he called. 'Wonderful view from here.'

Jessica looked uncertainly at the rigging. It was made from rope, criss-crossed into squares. These gave lots of footholds so it wouldn't be difficult to climb. But it was a long way up.

'Not nervous, are you?' called Great-Uncle Nelson.

'No! Of course not!' But her breath caught in her throat when she imagined herself, swaying in the empty air like a spider in a web.

She put her foot on the rope. Then both hands. Then the other foot. Then hand and foot, hand and foot, hand and foot, until the deck of the ship grew smaller and Uncle Nelson grew bigger. The breeze tugged at her clothes and hair, and she felt the rigging sway beneath her. She closed her eyes for a moment, to let the dizziness pass.

'Hurry up! Tea's getting cold.'

Jessica opened her eyes. It wasn't really all that much further. Great-Uncle Nelson seemed quite close. He looked down at her with a smile that was hidden by his bushy white beard. But she knew that he was smiling because his eyes were crinkled up. He reached down his short, fat arms to her.

Jessica climbed a little higher, until she felt her fingers clasped in Great-Uncle Nelson's hands. He hauled her up the last little bit of rigging and on to the narrow platform. There wasn't a lot of room so she had to stand quite close to him. But that was nice because he was a cuddly sort of person and smelled of apples.

Jessica reached up her hand and took hold of Great-Uncle Nelson's beard. She loved the feel of it: like cotton wool but grittier: cotton wool with bits in.

'I thought I'd have tea up here. I knew you'd come, so I brought enough for two.'

There was a handrail round three sides of the crow's nest. On it stood two mugs of tea and a plateful of cucumber sandwiches shaped like apples. Jessica knew that Grandma Liddell must have made them with her apple-shaped cutter.

Great-Uncle Nelson handed her one of the mugs and told her to help herself to sandwiches. She found that the bread was warm from the oven and the cucumber tangy with sea salt. It smelled as fresh and sharp as the breeze.

'Look at this,' said Great-Uncle Nelson. He took from his pocket a long blue telescope, decorated with silver moons and stars. He pulled it out to its full length and lifted it to his eye. He moved slowly round in a circle, scanning the whole horizon.

'Let me see. What can you see?' Jessica jumped up and down impatiently. 'Let me have a look.'

Great-Uncle Nelson lowered the telescope and passed it to her. At first she couldn't see anything.

'Over there,' he said, moving the telescope slowly round.

The telescope clicked and Jessica saw Grandma Liddell kneeling on the ocean bed, her grey hair coiled round her head in untidy plaits. Long wisps of hair had escaped from the plaits and the sea lifted them gently so that they looked like waving silver tendrils. Beside her was an enormous wooden chest with great brass hinges. The lid was open and Grandma Liddell was looking inside.

'It's a treasure chest,' breathed Jessica. 'A real treasure chest.' She imagined diamond necklaces, silver goblets, ruby earrings, brooches studded with emeralds, fat gold coins.

'Whose is it?' she whispered.

'It belongs,' said Great-Uncle Nelson, 'to Grandma and Grandpa Liddell, to your father, to Miss Darknight, and to all the Sweetapples. Including you.'

'Miss Darknight?' Jessica was horrified. 'How can it belong to Miss Darknight?'

'Because Euphemia is your Ancestor.'

Jessica couldn't speak. She must have misheard. She shook her head. 'No,' she whispered.

'Yes,' said Great-Uncle Nelson firmly. 'She's my sister.'

'Your sister?' Jessica looked out at the gently rolling sea. She didn't understand. 'But why isn't she in the ship? Why haven't you ever told me about her?'

'She chose the other place, Miasma, where the unhappy and angry go.'

Miasma. Jessica had heard of it: a terrible, terrifying place full of malevolent spirits and sobbing souls.

Jessica leaned against her uncle's warm arm and he put his hand on her head and stroked her hair.

'Why didn't you tell us she was coming? Couldn't you have warned us?'

'We've only just found out. There's no contact between the ship and Miasma. Miss Darknight must have crept across the seabed without anyone knowing, then on to the ship and into Apple Manor.'

And through the door to my bedroom, thought Jessica, with a shudder.

'But she answered Mother's advert for a new housekeeper,' Jessica thought out loud. 'She had an interview and Mother said she had good references.'

'Well, they wouldn't be difficult to forge, would they?' said Great-Uncle Nelson.

'What does she want?' Jessica slid down and sat on the floor of the crow's nest. She was beginning to understand how Mother felt: she hardly had the energy to stand. Great-Uncle Nelson crouched down beside her.

'Well, now: a long time ago, Apple Manor belonged to me. I inherited it as the elder child. I offered to share it, half and half with my sister, Euphemia Sweetapple. But she didn't want to share; she wanted it all. When I came to the ship I didn't have a child to bequeath it to and I was afraid to leave it to my sister. She always looked for the dark things. She would have ruined Apple Manor.' He shook his head sadly.

'She wasn't always like that: as children we used to play for hours together. When she got older things went badly for her. She became bitter and angry. She wanted to destroy. How could I give Apple Manor to someone like that?'

'Why can't she just go and leave us alone? It's not our fault that things went badly for her.'

The old man put his arm round the young girl's shoulder. 'Euphemia wants what she thinks is hers. She's prepared to do battle to get it. And if she can't have it, she'll destroy it.'

Jessica felt sick at her uncle's words. She imagined flashing swords and cannon fire, charging horses and red-coated soldiers. She imagined Miss Darknight bearing down on Apple Manor on a shining black horse, her black cloak flying behind her, and a sword held high at the end of her outstretched arm.

'Let battle commence,' said Nelson quietly to himself.

And then Jessica knew that battle had already commenced; that she had to be a warrior, whether she liked it or not. Somehow she had to get Miss Darknight to leave Apple Manor. Jessica sighed. She wished that the Special Child would come and take care of things.

'People like Euphemia are always engaged in battles of one sort or another,' her uncle said. 'But the Ancestors care about what happens. Don't you forget that.'

With shaky hands, she raised the telescope to her eye once more. She felt it click, then she saw Grandma Liddell pull a piece of paper from the trunk and take it over to her rocking-horse. She sat down and began to read, a smile of contentment spreading across her face.

Jessica sighed with frustration. She had to see what was inside that trunk! But she couldn't because Grandma had closed the lid. Perhaps the paper was a list of all the Ancestors' treasure! She tried to imagine the hoard of shimmering jewels that might lie inside the trunk.

She imagined herself in a glittering diamond tiara, just like a real princess; sometimes Great-Uncle Nelson called her his princess. Then she tried to imagine her mother wearing ruby earrings and drinking from a silver goblet. Grandpa Liddell would have a golden watch on a chain and Grandma would have an emerald brooch in the shape of an apple. Her father would have a fat gold watch that he could tuck away in his pocket.

'Is there a crown in there?' she asked. 'I should like to wear a crown.'

'It's not that sort of treasure,' her uncle replied. 'The chest is filled with real treasure, not crowns and jewels. Really, Jessica, you can sometimes be distressingly materialistic.'

Her heart sank. 'What's in there, then?' she asked.

Nelson put his hands on Jessica's shoulders and turned her to face him. He looked into her eyes and his expression was serious.

'Inside that trunk is a record of all the noble deeds carried out by all the Sweetapples who ever lived. It is a record of courage and selflessness; it is a great book of life.'

'That's not treasure, that's boring!' Tears sprang to her eyes and she felt her face go red.

Her uncle's arms folded round her in one of his big bear hugs. It felt nice. It felt warm. Then she had a thought. She shrugged her shoulders out of his arms. Was anything she'd ever done or said recorded in that chest? Probably not. She'd never been particularly brave, and her mother sometimes said she was selfish.

'I don't suppose I'm in there,' she said grumpily.

'Oh, I think there are quite a few sheets of paper with your name written on them. If I remember correctly.'

'What sort of thing?'

'If you think very carefully, I'm sure you'll remember for yourself those times when you've been extra kind or good.'

'There aren't very many,' she said crossly.

'Ah, there's the pity of it,' said her uncle with a sigh. 'Lost opportunities. Moments when we failed to be brave or kind. Happens to the best of us.'

Jessica couldn't imagine it happening to Great-Uncle Nelson or Grandma Liddell. They were always kind.

'Is Miss Darknight in there?' she asked, sure that she wouldn't be.

'Oh yes, Euphemia's in there, all right. Not as thick a pile as one might wish for, but she's definitely in there.'

'She can't be. She's horrible. I hate her!'

'Even people you hate are sometimes kind,' said Great-Uncle Nelson. 'Nobody's all bad.'

Jessica knew for an absolute one hundred per cent certainty that Miss Darknight *was* all bad.

'I think there's something else you should take a

look at while you're up here.' Great-Uncle Nelson took the telescope from her hand and put it to his eye. His face squinted and scrunched like an old, old apple. 'There we are,' he said. 'What can you see?'

It took her a while to focus properly and at first she couldn't see anything. Then the telescope clicked and absolutely clearly, Jessica saw.

5. Through the telescope

She saw Miss Darknight in Mother's room at Apple Manor. She was standing in front of the tall, thin mirror and wearing her mother's scarlet evening dress.

Jessica lowered the telescope and looked at Great-Uncle Nelson, her mouth open, her eyes shocked. But he didn't notice. He was eating the last of the cucumber sandwiches and gazing out to sea. She looked through the telescope once more.

Mother's dress was loose and baggy on thin Miss Darknight. But the woman seemed to think she looked beautiful. She gazed at her reflection in the mirror, turned this way and that, admired herself from different angles. She patted her hair.

'I am so very beautiful,' Jessica heard her say. 'Don't you think so, Captain Pottage?' She smiled at somebody. But there was no one there. She twirled round and round the big, blue bedroom in Mother's scarlet satin dress. Jessica grasped the telescope tightly. Her hands shook.

'You see, Captain Pottage,' Miss Darknight continued, 'Apple Manor will one day be mine, I shall see to that. I *am* seeing to that. Already Mr Sweetapple has gone. Apple Manor is rightfully mine. Mine! Mine! Mine!' Miss Darknight stamped her foot so hard that her sharp stiletto heels made marks in the wooden floor. Her red mouth twisted and her blue eyes glittered.

'All that mess. All that wood carving. And to have that dreadful child in the house; can you imagine it? One may as well keep pigs.

'The Sweetapples don't deserve to live in a beautiful house like Apple Manor. It's order and precision that are needed, Captain Pottage. Order and precision. And I shall impose it!' She stamped her foot again. Her eyes glittered like splintered ice. The satin dress shimmered.

'Of course Father made a mess!' cried Jessica. 'He's a wood carver. You have to make a mess to make beautiful things. Don't you see?' She remembered her father telling her that. She remembered him taking her on to his knee and explaining it all, just before he left.

She thought of the sweet smell of wood shavings scattered on the floor of Father's workroom. She thought of the blocks of wood that turned into beautiful things as he worked on them with his clever hands. Once he had carved a seahorse for her. A seahorse so beautiful and so full of life that she thought it might swim away from her, back to the ocean.

'You see, Jessie,' he had told her, 'the seahorse was in the block of wood all the time, waiting for me to uncover it. Every block of wood I use has inside it the thing that I'm going to make. It's my job to carve until I find that thing.'

Jessica knew that what her father said was true. 'He has to make sawdust and shavings before he can find the proper shape of things. Don't you see, Miss Darknight?'

But Miss Darknight didn't answer. Instead, the telescope clicked and took Jessica across the hallway of Apple Manor, past the grandfather clock and the Family Tree, up the wooden stairs and through the door of the little library.

It was filled with books. Two leather armchairs were set by the fire, and photographs of the Ancestors covered the top of an enormous desk. Sitting at the desk, wearing the scarlet satin dress, was Mother.

Jessica blinked and felt her eyelashes brush the rim of the telescope. 'I don't understand . . .'

'What don't you understand?' Great-Uncle Nelson was practising the Sailor's Hornpipe, but he was not the lightest or most graceful of dancers, and the little wooden platform shook. He almost knocked the telescope out of her hand when he pretended to climb the ship's rigging.

'Stop it, Uncle! You'll have us overboard!'

'Sorry, my dear. Have to keep fit, you know. It's a very stressful life being an Ancestor; trying to keep the family in order.' He took out a great, spotted handkerchief and wiped his face.

'Mother's wearing the red dress,' said Jessica, when her uncle's breathing was back to normal. 'Miss Darknight was wearing it a minute ago. What's going on?' Perhaps, she thought, Miss Darknight had one just the same. Perhaps she'd had a copy made.

'No, it's the same dress,' said Great-Uncle Nelson, reading her mind again.

'But Miss Darknight always wears black. Always.'

'Ah, but she's imagining a time when she'll be mistress of Apple Manor. She thinks she's in mourning now, you see: that's why she wears black.'

'In mourning?'

'For Apple Manor and what she's lost. She thinks she's been cheated of her rightful inheritance. When she gets Apple Manor she'll be able to wear red, green, or sky-blue-pink if she wants to.'

'But she won't get Apple Manor. She can't! Can she? What's she lost?'

Great-Uncle Nelson gave Jessica a hug. 'Questions, questions, questions, Jessie; what a questioner you are. There's a time for everything, and everything in its time.'

'*Why* won't you answer me? Why won't you say that she'll never have Apple Manor? Why won't you tell me that everything's OK?'

'Because it's not, is it?' he answered quietly.

No, thought Jessica; it's not.

'What about that telescope now?' said her uncle. 'What else can you see?'

Mother was writing a letter. The telescope zoomed closer. So close that she could read what her mother had written.

> *My Dear Husband,*
>   *How much longer will you be away? Have you*
> *found the special wood yet? We know that your quest is*
> *very important but Jessica and I miss you so much.*
> *Apple Manor is pining for you too. It creaks and groans*
> *like a stiff old man. It cries out in the night as if in pain.*

Her mother stood up and went to the corner of the room. Jessica saw, hidden behind one of the armchairs, another treasure chest. Perhaps this one would have real treasure in it.

Mrs Sweetapple drew a big iron key out of her pocket and inserted it in the padlock. The enormous lid creaked open, and Jessica saw that the chest was filled with old letters and photographs. She felt a thud of disappointment. She gazed sadly at her mother's back as it began to fade, then to disappear completely.

Jessica blinked and saw Miss Darknight leaning over the chest. Then the woman stood up and banged the lid shut, so that the wooden echo boomed in Jessica's ears.

Miss Darknight's face was red with rage: red as the scarlet dress. She rushed to the other side of the little library and, one by one, turned all the photographs of the Ancestors on to their faces. Then she picked up Mrs Sweetapple's letter from the desk and tore it into a hundred tiny pieces. She lifted her hands high into the air and let the pieces swirl, like snowflakes, to the floor.

But Euphemia Darknight was a tidy person. Immediately she stooped to pick them up again. When all the pieces had been picked from the carpet she looked round for somewhere to put them. Quickly she walked to the fireplace and sprinkled them into a vase on the mantelpiece.

'She's torn up Mother's letter! Did you see that? I'm going to tell Mother the minute I get back!'

'Well, actually, she hasn't written it yet,' said Great-Uncle Nelson.

'Yes she has! I just saw her with my own eyes!'

'No, my lamb. You saw her with the telescope's eye. Quite a different matter altogether.'

'What?' Jessica frowned. Sometimes her uncle talked in absolute riddles!

'Telescope time, Jess. It can see events which haven't happened yet. Other times it sees things which have already been and gone. And, if it's in a good mood, it might show us what's happening at that very moment.'

'Is it magic, then?'

'Some people might say so, I suppose.'

'How d'you know Mother hasn't written the letter yet?'

'Look.' Great Uncle Nelson pointed to the side of the telescope. There were three red lights that Jessica hadn't noticed. One was labelled 'time past', the second was labelled 'time present' and the third, 'time future'. The light for 'time future' flashed like a winking red eye.

'It's an event in the future, you see.'

Jessica nodded. 'I'd better see what Miss Darknight's doing in the future, then.'

She lifted the telescope and began to watch Miss Darknight again. She saw her go to her mother's desk and take out writing paper and an envelope. She began to write in angry red ink.

Husband,

 You have been gone so long, I hardly think it worthwhile your returning. Jessica and I are managing quite well without you. Miss Darknight is an absolute treasure; I really don't know what we'd do without her. We make such a happy trio here at Apple Manor that I wish you would go and find yourself a new wife and child.

 Yours insincerely,

 Carlotta Sweetapple,

 your no-longer-devoted wife

'No! She can't do that! You've got to stop her, Uncle.' But Jessica couldn't tear her eye away from the telescope. She watched as Miss Darknight shook her head.

 'What a silly Euphemia I am.' She smiled to herself, a crooked smile that twisted her face sideways. 'He'll see in a minute that the writing's not his *dearly beloved wife's*.' She spat the words out. Then she lifted her hand high above the letter and sprinkled something down upon it; something that looked like the small flakes of charred paper that swirl through the air from bonfires.

Jessica saw that once the flakes touched the letter, they completely disappeared. Then, spellbound, she watched the words of Miss Darknight's letter twist and squirm like little black worms. Once they had settled down, she realised that Miss Darknight's writing had changed into her mother's.

'I've got to get hold of that letter before she posts it,' said Jessica. 'If my father reads it he'll never come back.' Then a strange thought occurred to her. She turned to her uncle. 'How could she know to write that letter when Mother hasn't even written her own letter yet?'

'Miss Darknight's letter's not been written yet, either.'

'Oh.' Jessica frowned. 'This telescope mixes everything up.'

'Well, not really,' said Great-Uncle Nelson. 'It always gets the events right: absolutely right. It's just that sometimes it tells you about them before they've happened. It can be very useful actually. A bit like a weather forecast. Anyway, you don't think your father would believe a lot of nonsense like that, do you?'

Jessica didn't answer. She couldn't take her eyes off Miss Darknight.

At just that moment, the door to the library opened and in walked Mother. Miss Darknight turned quickly and wiped her hands on her skirt, as if they were sticky. Her letter had gone from the desk and she was wearing her usual black clothes again.

Mrs Sweetapple smiled at Miss Darknight. And, as she did so, she began to fade. She faded so much that Jessica could almost see through her. As her mother faded, Miss Darknight grew darker and darker.

'Mother! Come back!' Jessica called. 'Please come back.'

6. Knowledge is power

But Mrs Sweetapple hadn't disappeared completely. She walked across to the desk and Jessica found that she could see straight through her to the bookcases on the wall. She could see books in her skirt and books in her blouse. She looked like a ghost.

'Miss Darknight, have you seen my letter? I was writing a letter to Mr Sweetapple. I left it right here on the desk.'

'There you are, then; she has written it. Told you.' Jessica poked Great-Uncle Nelson in the ribs.

'I'm sure you've been in the kitchen all morning, Mrs Sweetapple. Are you quite sure you were writing a letter? Perhaps you were just thinking about writing one. If you don't mind my saying so, you've been very confused and forgetful just lately. Why don't you let me make you a nice cup of tea?'

Jessica saw her mother begin to tremble. Her face looked even paler than before. She put her hand on the back of the chair and said, in such a faint voice that Jessica had to put her ear to the telescope, 'Perhaps you're right. You're so kind, Miss Darknight. Yes, a nice cup of tea would be just the thing.' And Mrs Sweetapple sat down on the chair and put her head in her hands.

'Don't listen to her, Mother. She's lying. She's trying to make you think you're going mad, but you're not. You're not!'

Tears rolled down Jessica's cheeks. 'I have to get back to Mother. Miss Darknight's frightening her.'

'Your mother's stronger than you think, my dear.

There's a battle to be fought, that's for sure; but your mother's a fighter.'

'She might have been once, but not since Miss Darknight came to Apple Manor. I want to go back.'

'I know you do, my lamb; but it's not time for you to go yet.'

Great-Uncle Nelson towered over her. She looked up at him, at his white beard and crinkly eyes, and all of a sudden he seemed like a brick wall to her: solid and immoveable, absolutely sure of his place in the world. Almost before she knew what she was doing, she had hurled herself at him, her fists beating at his chest, her feet, in their strong black boots, kicking at his shins, his ankles, anything at all that got in their way.

'Let me go! You can't make me stay here.'

'Jessica, slow down, you'll hurt yourself. You'll go hurtling over the edge of the crow's nest if you're not careful.' Very gently, Great-Uncle Nelson took the telescope out of her hand and put his arms round her. He pinned her own arms by her side so that she couldn't move. As soon as they were still enough, he covered both of her feet with one of his own very large ones; firmly enough to pin them down, but not so that it hurt.

'I hate you!'

'Sweetheart, if you want to go home, then of course you can. Just let me explain that the telescope hasn't finished yet. Can't you feel it still buzzing?' He put the telescope against her cheek.

She felt a very faint vibration. She kept her face pressed against it; she felt suddenly tired and the buzzing sensation was soothing. She could almost have fallen asleep.

'Didn't I just say that there's a time for everything, Jessie? The telescope has things for you to see, and you must see them while they're still there. Nobody knows why the telescope works when it does; it might not work again for another fifty years. Come on, let's see what else you can see through there.'

Jessica shivered. She was afraid of what she might see.

'What d'you think, Jessie?'

She nodded and took the telescope from Great-Uncle Nelson.

Miss Darknight had returned and was holding out a steaming cup of tea to Mrs Sweetapple.

'About the letter,' she said. 'I saw Jessica in here earlier. She was reading something on the desk. If you ask me, that young lady needs taking in hand.'

'It is very difficult,' she heard her mother saying. 'With her father away and everything. She misses him so much, you see.'

'Stuff and nonsense! Begging your pardon, Mrs Sweetapple, but I believe in plain speaking.'

'Of course, Miss Darknight.' Mother's voice was so faint that Jessica had to strain to hear it.

'And it seems to me,' Miss Darknight continued, 'that if you did write a letter, and I'm not saying that you did and I'm not saying that you didn't, but if you did write a letter, then I wouldn't put it past that daughter of yours to steal it. Steal it or rip it into a thousand tiny pieces.' Miss Darknight made small tearing movements with her hands.

'Oh, I'm sure Jessica wouldn't . . .'

'You don't know the half of it,' said Miss Darknight.

'But she . . .'

'Not the half!'

'What shall I do?' Mother whispered.

'Just leave it to me,' said Miss Darknight, in a voice as soft as rotting apples. 'I think I know how to deal with that daughter of yours.'

'You can't have Apple Manor, d'you hear? You're not having it. It's ours. Not yours. Ours!' Jessica stamped her foot over and over again until it tingled, and the platform of the crow's nest shuddered.

'Whoa, Jessie.'

'I'm not a horse!'

'You stamp like one.' Great-Uncle Nelson put his hand on her shoulder. She shrugged it off.

'That's it, Jessie. That's all the telescope wants to tell us for now. Knowledge is power, my dear; it gives you some ammunition at least.'

'*Oh, yes*. I've got a great big pile of hand grenades under my bed. And I mustn't forget the water pistol in the shed. I've got *loads* of ammunition, I don't think.'

Great-Uncle Nelson smiled a little sadly. 'You know what Miss Darknight's up to. That's the most important thing. You must watch and pray.'

Watch and pray. She couldn't help watching and, ever since the day Father left, she'd been praying that Miss Darknight would go. She wished the legend of the Special Child were true: Apple Manor needed someone powerful.

Great-Uncle Nelson pulled the great red and white spotted handkerchief out of his pocket. It was as big as a tablecloth. He put it to Jessica's face and gently wiped her eyes. She hadn't even realised she'd been crying. He bent down and gave her a noisy kiss on her forehead. His beard brushed against her nose and tickled it.

'Ah – ah – ah – ah – chooooooo!' Jessica's sneeze was so big that it knocked the sandwich plate clean off the rail of the crow's nest. The plate flipped over and over, all the way down to the deck where it exploded into a thousand pieces. She watched, fascinated, as the pieces flew in all directions.

'Hey, mind what you're doing up there!' Out from under the canvas tarpaulin of a lifeboat crawled Grandpa Liddell. 'Can't a feller have fifty winks without the world going mad? I ask you!'

'I thought it was forty winks,' said Jessica.

'Grandpa Liddell prefers fifty,' replied Great-Uncle Nelson.

'Grandpa! Look up here!' Jessica was so pleased to see him that she jumped up and down on the small platform.

'Watch out! You'll have the mugs over the side next, if you're not careful. You're suddenly feeling better, young lady.'

'It's because I've seen Grandpa,' smiled Jessica.

'Hmph! Had enough of your old Sweetapple, I suppose.'

'You're like jam doughnuts, Uncle. I couldn't ever have enough of you.'

'What are you doing up there?' called Grandpa. 'Did that rascal Sweetapple talk you into it?'

'Yes!' Jessica answered. 'He did!' She turned and grinned up at Great-Uncle Nelson.

'What do you mean, yes?' grumbled her uncle. 'How dare he call me a rascal? He's a doddery old sea dog.'

'I didn't mean that *I* think you're a rascal.'

'I should hope not too. Anyway, we'd better get down now. Your grandma will have something cooking.'

'But you've only just eaten all those sandwiches. And I didn't even have one.'

'What's that got to do with anything?' asked Great-Uncle Nelson crossly. 'Can't a chap be hungry when he wants?'

'I suppose.'

Jessica looked over the edge of the crow's nest. The thought of moving away from the safety of the platform made her feel dizzy.

'You've gone a funny colour,' said Great-Uncle Nelson. 'Don't fancy the climb down, eh?'

Jessica shook her head.

'Don't worry. I'll give you a fireman's lift.' He clattered the mugs together in his hand.

Jessica frowned. 'How did you get up here?' she

asked. 'With two mugs of tea and a plateful of sandwiches?'

'Ha ha! I wondered when you'd think about that.' Great-Uncle Nelson pulled the telescope from his pocket. 'Watch.'

He pulled the telescope one way, then another. The moon and stars disappeared and strange-looking pieces of metal and canvas appeared instead. He pushed one of the pieces of metal upwards so that it opened out like an umbrella, although it was more bowl shaped than anything. Then, to Jessica's astonishment, Great-Uncle Nelson put the bowl on his head. A piece of elastic hung to one side of his face and he pulled it down, tucked it under his chin, and fastened it to the other side of the bowl. The bowl was a hat!

The hat had four pieces of metal sticking out: one at each side and one each at the front and the back. They looked like rulers. Each piece of metal had a hook at the end. Great-Uncle Nelson hung the mugs from two of the hooks; one at either side of his ears.

Jessica giggled. 'You look funny,' she said.

'Nonsense,' said Great-Uncle Nelson. 'It's a perfectly practical device. Everyone should have one.'

'But how did you stop the tea from spilling?'

'I put the mugs here.' His hand moved round the edge of his hat, pulling out a sort of ledge as it did so. Now the hat had an enormous brim, as wide as a tea-tray. Here he put the mugs.

'What happens if they fall off?'

'Jessica Sweetapple, you are a girl full of questions today. You are bursting at the seams with questions.'

Great-Uncle Nelson took one of the mugs from the rim of his hat. 'Observe,' he said, tipping the mug upside down, 'the magnetic base.'

'No wonder it was so heavy,' said Jessica. 'But what about the plate? Did you have to balance that on your head?'

'In a manner of speaking,' said Great-Uncle Nelson. 'Observe once more.'

'Are you two coming?' called Grandpa Liddell from below.

'Tell him he's a silly old fool and I'll be down in my own good time.'

Jessica giggled. 'I can't tell him that.'

'Just ignore him, then. Now, shall I show you where the plate goes or not? Observe, if you will, the arrangement of four elastic straps.' Great-Uncle Nelson pulled the straps from a hole at the top of the hat. Each strap had a metal clip at its end.

'We will have to imagine a plate as we no longer have one, owing to the fact that somebody smashed it. Mentioning no names, of course.'

Jessica blushed.

'The plate balances on the top of my head, like so. The four straps are pulled underneath it and clip on to the edge of the plate. The whole thing is then perfectly balanced and beautifully stable. Rather like myself in fact. Now, shall we go?'

Suddenly Jessica seemed to be flying through the air, as Great-Uncle Nelson lifted her over his shoulder in a fireman's lift. She closed her eyes as she felt the movement of him swinging out over the edge of the crow's nest, and then beginning the long climb back down the rigging. Her head bumped gently against his back with soft, rhythmic thuds.

When they reached the deck, Grandpa Liddell lifted her from Great-Uncle Nelson's shoulders and put her over his own. 'About time too,' he said. 'Grandma's got dinner ready.'

7. Door to the past

Down they went, down into the bowels of the ship, down below the waterline where the timbers creaked, where the air smelled of tar and old rope, and where the forgotten words of long-ago sailors rumbled through the hold.

Grandpa Liddell worked his way round wooden barrels stacked higher than a man until, at last, he came to the Ancestors' Door. The door opened inwards but the sea did not follow. It glided past like the well-behaved ocean it was, carrying seahorses, starfish and, of course, the Ancestors. Jessica heard the familiar creaking sound of Grandma Liddell's rocking-horse.

She stretched out her arms and let herself fall slowly forward into the blue-green waters of the warm sea. It wasn't wet. It didn't get into her eyes or mouth. She didn't breathe it in. It felt like the ripple of soft warm silk against her skin. Her fears of Miss Darknight and for Apple Manor slipped quietly away.

'I'm off to check the seating arrangements,' said Grandpa Liddell mysteriously. 'Grandma put me in charge.' He threw his chest out proudly like a small boy, and swam away round the bow of the ship.

'There you are, Jessica!'

'Granny Harriet!' Jessica swam quickly to the old woman's side and threw her arms round her neck.

Granny Harriet had been one of Florence Nightingale's nurses during the Crimean War and had lots of stories to tell. Becoming a mother had been tiresome, she'd once told Jessica, for she much preferred nursing wounded soldiers to nursing babies, although she'd had eleven in the end, so she must have liked them really. Personally, Jessica preferred gerbils.

'Tell me more stories about the wounded soldiers you looked after.'

'Bored with wounded soldiers, child. Bored, bored, bored! I'm fed up with living in this place with all these bickering folk. Can't even get away from my own children! Bored! I'm ready for the Great Sleep.'

'Is it time?' Jessica asked.

'Who knows?' said Granny Harriet gloomily. 'It's not for us to know the time or the place. But it must be soon. Must be.'

Jessica put her hand gently on Granny's shoulder. The Great Sleep was something all the Ancestors looked forward to; it was a time of reward for all the hard work and tiredness of life. And then, after a very long time indeed, nobody knew how long, not even Grandma Liddell, there would be the Joyous Awakening.

'I'll come and visit you,' said Jessica.

'No point. No point at all. Won't know about it, will I?'

'I suppose not,' said Jessica. She shivered. It wasn't like Granny Harriet to be so bad-tempered and gloomy.

'Off you go, child,' said Granny Harriet. 'Go and say hello to the other old fogies.'

'Will you be all right?'

Granny Harriet tushed and waved her handkerchief at Jessica. 'Don't fuss so, child. You're just like old Florrie Nightingale. Although she was much more tart than you: a Granny Smith to your Golden Delicious. Off you go now; see who else you can see.'

Jessica kissed Granny Harriet, then turned on her back and let the gentle current carry her towards her great-grandmother. Soon she came to the old woman's rocking-horse. It pulled a great wooden sleigh that had two leather seats which faced each other.

'Ah, there you are, Jessica,' smiled Grandma Liddell. She was seated in a corner of the sleigh with a tartan blanket thrown across her knees. She swayed with the rhythm of the horse as it creaked and rocked on the sandy floor of the seabed.

Jessica paddled towards her so that she could sit on her knee and put her arms round the old woman's neck. She laid her head on her breast. She felt the smooth black bombasine of her dress and heard the steady beating of her heart. She felt the rise and fall of her breathing, like the ebb and flow of the sea. Jessica's eyes closed.

'Tell me what's happening at Apple Manor, child.' Grandma's wrinkled old hand stroked Jessica's head. It felt so good that Jessica didn't want to speak. She wanted the rocking and the stroking to go on and on.

'Tell me.'

When she had finished the sleepy telling of it all, she heard Grandma Liddell sigh.

'I thought as much. Those in the Great Sleep are restless.' Grandma laced her fingers more firmly across Jessica's back. 'Sir Lancelot and Lady Imogen have been stirring on their tombs: a great creaking and groaning and snoring.'

'Can I go to see them?'

'Of course. We are all going. We must be there to greet Sir Lancelot and Lady Imogen when they wake. Everyone's a-chatter and a-quiver with it.'

'Why?' asked Jessica, who had never been to an Awakening.

'Because,' said Grandma, 'in the Book of the Prophets it is written that Sir Lancelot and Lady Imogen will end their Great Sleep when Apple Manor begins to shake and to weep and to crumble. The Manor will be saved by a Special Child who will be empowered by Sir Lancelot.'

'But there is no Special Child. All the children are gone except me. Apple Manor's going to fall to the ground and there's nothing anyone can do.' Jessica sat up and clutched at Grandma's shoulders. 'What are we going to do?'

'Apple Manor has stood for a thousand years, Jessica. It will stand for a thousand more.' Jessica looked into the old woman's sweet, gnarled face. 'You'll see,' said Grandma. 'You'll see.'

Suddenly there was a great movement of water

that lifted Jessica's hair so that it waved around her head like a moving halo. It was Great-Uncle Nelson, galoshing along the seabed so that everything rocked as if it had been caught in the wake of a ship. The great galleon swayed gently from side to side and Jessica could imagine the bow creaking and shifting against her bedroom wall. Sometimes, at night, the sound of it woke her and she wondered what the Ancestors were up to.

'Is there no food to be had anywhere? Is a man to starve after generations of service to his family? Is there no gratitude? Does no one *care* that I am about to expire from starvation?'

'Yes, no, no, no, in that order,' said Grandma Liddell. 'Really, Nelson, you're like a great big baby. Goodness knows what you were like when you *were* a baby. Your mother must have torn her hair out.'

'Certainly not,' said Great-Uncle Nelson. 'She has a marvellous head of hair, as well you know. You will see it at dinner-time. That is if we ever get any dinner.'

'The Ancestor Feast will be held *after* the Awakening,' said Grandma Liddell. 'There would hardly be any point if the chief guests were not there. Can't you wait like everyone else?'

'Are we in the Banqueting Hall?' asked Jessica.

'Of course,' said Grandma. 'Where else would we be for an Ancestor Feast?'

'Great!'

'You'll have to save me a place at the table,' said Great-Uncle Nelson Sweetapple. 'That old double-crossing, feather-brained Liddell won't have remembered me, you can be sure of that. Sure as eggs is eggs. You just make sure I get fed, Jessie. Somebody's got to spare a thought for me. Starve otherwise.' He pulled out a huge, tablecloth hanky and wiped his eyes.

Jessica swam towards her uncle and helped him. He had to bend down so that she could reach.

'I spare lots of thoughts for you. Lots of them. And they're nearly all about how lovely you are and how much I love you.'

Great-Uncle Nelson burst into tears all over again and Jessica wondered what she'd said to upset him.

'Hear that, Liddell, you old scoundrel? Hear that?

Your great-granddaughter loves me. Loves me! Or are you so busy fifty winking you can't hear anything?'

'Actually, he's doing the place settings,' said Jessica.

'Oh well, that's it then. There won't be a place for me, you can bet your bottom dollar.'

'I haven't got a bottom dollar,' said Jessica.

'Jessica Sweetapple?' called Grandma Liddell. 'Come here and let me brush your hair. It's time to meet the Ancestors.'

Jessica swam towards her grandmother. At last she would enter the Sea of the Great Sleep. At last she would see the tombs of her Sleeping Ancestors.

Something mysterious and magical was about to happen.

8. The Sea of the Great Sleep

The Ancestors trailed across the seabed in a great winding throng. The sea itself rippled with excitement. Jessica had heard that the Sea of the Great Sleep was rather like a country churchyard, except that there was no church and the tombs were all beneath the waves.

At last, the column of Ancestors began to slow down as it reached the place where Sir Lancelot and

Lady Imogen slept. The column broke up as Ancestors began to surround the tomb and soon Jessica realised she was too far back to see anything.

Putting her head down, she began to push her way through the throng of bodies that blocked her view. It wasn't easy: the push of the sea heaved against her, as if it was trying to push her even further back. Most Ancestors moved to let her pass, but some tutted and complained about the bad manners of modern youth. Eventually though, after much shoving and weaving and winding, she found herself in front of the tomb.

At first it seemed to Jessica that nothing was happening. Sir Lancelot and Lady Imogen lay side by side, marble eyes gazing heavenward, hands pushed together in prayer. But her mouth dropped open at what she saw next: Lady Imogen's toe gave a definite wiggle.

Jessica stared hard. Nothing moved. Then she noticed that the marble was cracking; very fine, hairline cracks, like those on the shell of an egg. It was like waiting for a chick to hatch.

More movements. An elbow, a foot, somebody's

arm. Sir Lancelot turned his head and there was a sharp crack. The two ancient Ancestors began to toss from side to side and the fissures in the marble grew wider with each movement.

Sir Lancelot snored loudly and his marble nose vibrated. A great gasp went up from the Ancestors as a particularly violent snore dislodged the nose entirely, and it floated gently down to the seabed.

Lady Imogen turned over and sighed. She prodded her husband in the ribs with her elbow. 'Really, Lancelot, I keep telling you not to lie on your back. You know it makes things worse. I've had just about enough. I'm getting up.'

'Oh, Immy, come back and lie down.'

'No, Lancelot, we can't go back to sleep, we're needed at Apple Manor. We've been called. And besides, look at the state we're in.' Lady Imogen struggled to sit up, causing a thousand tiny cracks to race across the marble's surface.

With a great crashing and creaking, Sir Lancelot and Lady Imogen sat up together. The marble fell from their bodies. A milky-white cloud of dust swirled around and above them, so that for a moment Jessica lost sight of them completely. But then, as the dust fell slowly to the ocean floor, she saw them pushing the clumps of marble from their bodies to send a small avalanche hurtling down from the tomb.

'Immy! Immy, quick! My neck, I can't move it.' Sir Lancelot winced as Lady Imogen started to rub his shoulders and neck. 'Got a crick in it.'

'Hardly surprising after nearly a thousand years, my darling. I'm feeling a bit stiff myself.' Lady Imogen massaged her husband's neck.

'Down a bit. Just there, yes. Now up a bit. To the right a bit more. Yes, that's it. Oooh! Oooh, that's lovely.' Sir Lancelot shuddered and let out a great sigh. He was actually quite distinguished looking, Jessica thought, with his twirly silver moustache and beautiful, silver, thick hair.

And she was surprised to see how young and pretty Lady Imogen was. She gasped with delight at her Ancestor's long white dress, trimmed with gold braid and covered with gold and silver stars. Her hair was long and as shiny-red as leaves in autumn.

Jessica noticed that Sir Lancelot seemed to have forgotten about his stiff neck. He was gazing around him with a look of pure astonishment on his face. 'Lady Imogen,' he whispered.

'What is it, my dear? You look quite pale. You look as if you've seen a ghost.'

'They've all come, Immy. Look at them. All our babies. They've all come to see us, to greet us, to welcome us from the Great Sleep.' Two tears, like drops of crystal, rolled down his face. He held out his arms as if to embrace everyone. 'My babies! My babies!' he called.

But then Sir Lancelot seemed to notice that 'his babies' made up a very large audience, all watching him sit on his tomb and wax sentimental. He blushed and cleared his throat. 'Well, haven't I always said that if you bring them up properly, they'll turn out right in the end. "Give me a child until he's seven", and all that.' He cleared his throat again and coughed. 'Well, can't stay here all day. Things to do, people to see.' And with a great clanking of chain mail and armour, he heaved himself to the side of the tomb.

'Allow me, oh many-greated grandfather.' Great-Uncle Nelson held out both hands to help Sir Lancelot down.

Sir Lancelot stood back and looked at Great-Uncle Nelson. Then a smile of recognition swept across his face and he threw his arms round Nelson Sweetapple and hugged him. 'Look at him, bless him. My own great-great-great-great . . .' (the greats went on for some time) 'grandson. Look at his lovely little face.' Sir Lancelot chucked Uncle Nelson's cheek. 'You're a grand little chap, Nelson. I'm so proud of you.'

'Lancelot, for goodness sake; he's seventy-five if he's a day. Nearly twice as old as you were before you came to the ship. Get a grip on yourself; he's not a baby.' Lady Imogen glared beautifully at her husband.

'Here, take no notice of Immy, she's never very good when she gets up in the morning. Take this groat and buy yourself an ice-cream with it; but don't let the others know or they'll all be wanting one. Haven't got money to burn, you know.' Sir Lancelot put his hand behind his breastplate and drew out a small leather pouch.

Great-Uncle Nelson took out his handkerchief and blew his nose. He put the groat carefully into his pocket, next to his gold watch and chain. 'D'you mind if I get a strawberry ice-lolly instead?' he asked.

Suddenly Jessica felt herself pushed from behind.

'An orderly queue, please! Let's form an orderly queue!' Sir Oscar Sweetapple, the bossiest Sweetapple in all creation, was trying to form the milling Ancestors into a line. Sir Herbert Sweetapple stood at the top of the line because he was the most ancient Ancestor, apart from Sir Lancelot and Lady Imogen, his father and mother.

'Really old Ancestors at the top, please! Those who came into the ship more recently should be further down! Grandparents before grandchildren, etcetera.' Sir Oscar marched up and down the line, checking names against a list, prodding people into their right places.

'Cheeky young whippersnapper,' said Grandma Liddell. 'Hardly been in the ship five minutes himself!'

'All those years shouting at soldiers in the army,'

said Grandpa. 'He probably thinks that's the normal way to talk to people.'

'Well it's not!' said Grandma crossly. 'And any Sweetapple worthy of the name shouldn't need a list to know who's who! That's what I think!'

'I don't want to go to the end of the line,' said Jessica. 'Can't I stay here with you?' She took hold of Grandpa's hand and held on to it tightly.

'I think we can ignore that bossy young Oscar,' said Grandpa. He gave her hand a gentle squeeze and Jessica smiled.

The line was so long that she couldn't see the end of it. She had to wait some time before she caught a glimpse of Sir Lancelot and Lady Imogen once more. They came slowly down the line, shaking hands, smiling, hugging, chatting. Ladies dabbed at their eyes with lace handkerchiefs and men cleared their throats loudly. Some, like Great-Uncle Nelson, were quite happy to cry as noisily as possible.

Jessica felt her heart thumping with excitement. Excitement, yes, but nervousness too. Lady Imogen was so beautiful that Jessica adored her already. She wanted to touch her milky-white skin to see if it really did feel like silk. She wanted those huge brown eyes to look at her. She wanted to be smiled at, to be noticed by her. It was like waiting for the Queen.

Grandpa looked down at her and smiled. 'Nervous?'

Jessica nodded.

'Well, try to stop fidgeting, there's a good girl.'

Jessica realised then that she'd been twisting this way and that, leaning forward to get a better view, jumping up and down as the excitement became all too much for her. She would try to be calm and to stand still. She would try to be as calm as Lady Imogen.

They were getting nearer. They were almost here. Lady Imogen kissed Great-Uncle Nelson on the cheek and wiped his eyes with her very own handkerchief. Jessica sighed.

Now they were talking to Grandma and Grandpa Liddell. Jessica could hardly bear it. She wanted it to be all over and done with. But she also knew that when it was, she would long to turn back the clock and for it to happen all over again.

They were talking about Apple Manor. Sir Lancelot wanted to know what was happening. Grandpa Liddell pulled her gently forward. 'If you really want to know all the details, Sir Lancelot, the best person to ask is young Jessica here.'

And then Sir Lancelot looked at her. His face turned pale and his eyes grew wide.

Jessica fidgeted nervously. What had she done? Was her hair a mess? Perhaps Sir Lancelot was disappointed with her. Perhaps she wasn't good enough to be the very youngest Sweetapple.

She couldn't take her eyes off Sir Lancelot, even though her face was red with shame and she could feel tears pricking dangerously at her eyes. What had she done?

Sir Lancelot took Lady Imogen's hand.

'Imogen. Imogen, look, my dear. It's the Special Child.'

9. The Special Child

'Come on, Jessica. Everyone's waiting to see the Special Child.' Sir Lancelot held her hand and began to walk across the seabed towards the Banqueting Hall. Lady Imogen was at her other side and Jessica almost fainted with pride at the feel of her hand inside the great lady's. Could she really be the Special Child? Was it true?

The Banqueting Hall was an enormous cave which

glowed with the light of a thousand candles. Although water surrounded them, they burned as brightly as if they burned in air. They were set on ledges around the uneven walls, and in chandeliers hanging from the high cave roof.

Down the centre of the cave stood a long, long table. It disappeared from view as it entered caverns and followed the twists and turns of a thousand passages. The table was set with yet more candles and great glass bowls of fruit, with knives and forks and glasses that glinted as they caught the light of the candles.

It was into this place that Sir Lancelot and Lady Imogen led the Special Child. The rest of the Ancestors were already seated at the great table and, to Jessica's great embarrassment, they applauded her as she entered. There must have been hundreds of them.

She wanted to see again those Ancestors who meant so much to her; if Sir Lancelot wanted special people, there were plenty of them here. She could see Sir Herbert Sweetapple, who'd fought alongside King

Harold at the Battle of Hastings. He liked to wear his chain mail and helmet at the Ancestor Feasts because he didn't want anyone forgetting what he'd done in life. During the Battle of Hastings he had ducked and the arrow which was meant for him had caught King Harold in the eye instead. He didn't win any medals but he was always boasting about how he changed the course of history.

'Come along, Jessica my dear. Everybody's waiting for you.' Sir Lancelot smiled kindly down at her. Jessica blushed as she realised the bugler had been forced to play the Sweetapple Anthem for a second time while everybody waited for her to finish daydreaming. She looked at the floor as they went to take their seats.

They formed a small procession, with Sir Lancelot at the front, followed by Lady Imogen and finally Jessica. As they approached the head of the table, she saw three gilded thrones draped in red velvet. The one in the centre was larger and grander than the two at either side. It was raised on a platform and six golden steps led up to it. She expected that Sir

Lancelot would sit there, or perhaps Lady Imogen. But no, with a sweep of his hand, Sir Lancelot indicated that this seat was Jessica's.

She felt herself blush again. It felt all wrong to be sitting in the most important seat of all. She loved the legend of the Special Child but how could it be her? She was just plain old Jessica Sweetapple who was made fun of by the wooden children at school, who missed her father and her friends, and who sometimes lost her temper and stamped her foot. What was so special about that?

But once she had climbed the steps and was seated, the throne felt so wonderful she didn't care if she was a Special Child or not. Its red velvet lining was so soft that she couldn't help running her fingers over and over and over it. She couldn't see Sir Lancelot or Lady Imogen at either side of her because the throne was so deep. She tucked her legs beneath her and sat right at the very back of it.

She heard the Apple Manor String Quartet playing mediaeval music. Outside, the bugler played variations on the Sweetapple Anthem and Jessica felt her heart swell with love for her ancient family and for Apple Manor. The sweeping silver notes made her want to stand up and raise her arms, to lift her head to the heavens, to tap her feet on the seabed and dance to the familiar, beloved music.

Suddenly there was a great roaring and cheering from the Ancestors. Jessica peered round the edge of the throne to see what was going on.

Grandma Liddell was walking down the length of the cave towards the High Table close to the entrance. She was followed by four child Ancestors bearing a roasted boar on a silver plate. The boar had an apple resting in its open mouth.

Everyone stood up and applauded Grandma Liddell. She nodded her head modestly and took her place at the High Table, in between Grandpa and Great-Uncle Nelson. They were right in front of the thrones and Grandma turned to wave at Jessica. She waved back and wished she could sit at the table with her very favourite and most loved Ancestors.

It was just as she was deciding how best to tell Sir Lancelot that he'd made a mistake – the Special Child was somebody else – that her food arrived on a golden tray.

Jessica took the tray and put it across her knees. She lifted the lid of the first dish and found it filled with golden pumpkin soup. This was followed by fish and vegetables, then a great mix of salads, then roast boar or roast venison (she noticed that Great-Uncle Nelson had both), then apricot sorbet followed by Apple Manor Pie served with thick golden cream and all finished up with coffee and mead.

Jessica pushed the tray as far away from her as she could, then curled up inside the throne and groaned with the weight of all the food she'd eaten. All around her the Ancestors talked and laughed and wept and laughed and argued and shouted and talked. Uncle Nelson declared that it was the first square meal he'd had in months, no thanks to Grandpa Liddell who'd have cheated him out of it given half the chance, no question about it.

Her mind wandered: images of her colourful family dancing and laughing, arguing, crying. It settled on her mother and father and she saw them together in Apple Manor, watching her. How proud they would be of her now, if they could really see her. She imagined their smiles, their hands on her head. She loved them so much. She wished they could come to the ship.

She felt her eyelids drooping. But even as they closed she felt, beneath the gossip and the laughter, something else. Something that coiled itself round every person in that ancient cave, that made its way through myriad passages to reach the very farthest, most distant Ancestor. It curled its way up inside the throne where she lay, and wound itself round her heart.

She sat up quickly, suddenly afraid. She thought of Miss Darknight and shivered. It was as though a black cloud had filled the cave. She almost jumped out of her skin as the boom of a gong reverberated throughout the cave and echoed along the passages. She heard the voice of Sir Oscar Sweetapple calling for silence and she peered round the edge of the throne so that she could see what was happening. She found that Sir Lancelot and Lady Imogen had done the same and all three of them sat in a row, watching Sir Oscar's face.

'The darkness is come!' Sir Oscar banged a hammer on the table for emphasis. 'The forces of evil are ranged against the body of Apple Manor and against the very foundations of the Sweetapple family. If we do not act now, then Apple Manor is doomed. Every Ancestor will have his Great Sleep and Joyous Awakening threatened.'

'Shame!' muttered Granny Harriet. 'Jolly bad shame. Body needs a bit of Great Sleep.'

'We must support the Special Child in every way we can. We must pray for her constantly.'

The rest of the Ancestors nodded and murmured and muttered.

Jessica felt dizzy. The air seemed to sway around her. Whispering voices muttered in her ear. *Darkness. Evil. Apple Manor.*

10. The empowering ceremony

Behind the thrones, a row of steps led upwards to a platform draped in red velvet embroidered with golden apples. Jessica's knees shook with fear as she followed Sir Lancelot and Lady Imogen to the top. She placed her feet carefully so that she wouldn't tread on Lady Imogen's beautiful dress which flowed down the steps like a silken river of white and gold.

At the top of the steps Jessica turned and looked

out at the faces of her Ancestors. She saw fear there, and something else too. She saw that they believed in her, that they trusted her, that they really did think she was the Special Child. She felt so small, smaller than she'd ever felt.

Flanking her, Sir Lancelot and Lady Imogen both reached out for her hands. She felt the warmth of their comforting fingers and she found the courage to look up into Lady Imogen's face.

'I'm not the Special Child,' she whispered. 'I'm not.' And then, to her horror, she burst into tears. In front of all those hundreds of people she stood there, feeling like a baby and convinced that she looked like an idiot. It only made matters worse when she heard the sympathetic 'tuts' and 'ohs' and 'ahs' of the adults. In fact it made her angry.

Lady Imogen and Sir Lancelot bent down to comfort her. Lady Imogen took a beautiful white silk handkerchief from the purse at her side and dabbed at Jessica's eyes.

'I know you don't *want* to be the Special Child, Jessica, but I'm afraid that you are.'

'Well, I'm not afraid,' said Sir Lancelot. 'I'm jolly pleased. Couldn't have produced a better Special Child if I'd invented her myself. Could I, now?'

'I'm still not the Special Child, though,' she whispered. 'It's no use pretending I am. You're special.'

Lady Imogen bent and kissed her on the cheek. Jessica lifted her hand to her face as if she wanted to hold the kiss in place for ever.

'Come on, Jess,' said Sir Lancelot. 'Time for the ceremony.'

Jessica heard the strains of the Sweetapple Anthem once more. She looked towards the mouth of the cave and a child Ancestor entered it, holding a cushion in front of him. The cushion held something sparkling.

'What is it?' Jessica whispered.

Sir Lancelot smiled at her. 'Ahh, just watch.'

The cushion-bearer was followed by a procession of musicians: the bugler, a violinist, a trumpeter, a harpist whose harp was mounted on a wheeled platform and pushed by another child Ancestor, a flautist, a drummer and a tuba player.

The procession stopped at the foot of the

platform. The music stopped too. Jessica saw that all the Ancestors had their faces turned towards her. She was the very centre of attention. And she didn't like it much.

'My dear descendents,' Sir Lancelot's voice boomed deep around the cave. Jessica wondered how he managed to do it. Even the tuba player was impressed. 'Lady Imogen and myself have woken from the Great Sleep because of the threat both to Apple Manor and to the entire Sweetapple dynasty. Our task is to empower the Special Child, so that she may save Apple Manor.

'She alone, Jessica Louisa Maud Sweetapple, can cross the threshold that separates the ship from Apple Manor. Her father, Sir Richard Sweetapple, whom many of you will remember from his visits to the ship as a child, is seeking the wood for our figurehead. On him depends the physical life of our ancestral home. But it is to Jessica Sweetapple that we look to fight the great battle between good and evil. On her depends the spiritual life of Apple Manor.'

Sir Lancelot looked down at her, his expression

serious. 'Jessica, you will be afraid. But you will succeed. With our blessings and prayers, with your special empowerment, you will succeed.'

Jessica tugged at Lady Imogen's sleeve. 'Is it all right to be scared, then?'

'It's perfectly all right, my dear. In fact if you weren't afraid I should think you weren't very sensible.'

'But what have I got to do?'

'You will discover that when you get to Apple Manor. Sometimes, at times of crisis or great need, the telescope allows us to see what is happening. But really it is not for the Ancestors to know the details of life beyond the ship; we sense only the great movements of good and evil. When the time comes you will find the right thing to do.'

Jessica was beginning to feel annoyed again. It was all right telling her she would know what to do when the time came. It was all right telling her she'd have no problem sorting things out once she got back to Apple Manor. It was all right for them! Her thoughts were interrupted by a roll of the drum. The voice of the bugler called: 'Bearer, mount the platform!'

The child Ancestor began to climb the steps. He held his arms stretched out in front of him, bearing the cushion. The drum beat in time to his slow footsteps.

Sir Lancelot reached towards the cushion and picked up a chain of glass beads. He turned to Jessica and she felt her heart race. She looked into his face and felt that there was just him and herself in the whole universe.

Then he held his hands apart so that she could see the chain properly. Lights of red and blue and green flashed from the beads and the colour seemed to flow in a circuit through the chain.

'What you see are streams of living water,' said Sir Lancelot. And as he said it Jessica felt as if that living water was coursing and pulsing through her own veins.

At the centre of the chain was a magnificent crystal apple. Suspended inside the apple were its crystal core and crystal pips. The apple pulsed with light.

Sir Lancelot lifted the chain into the air. 'With the power vested in me as Most Ancient Ancestor, I empower our beloved descendent, the Special Child of the Generations, Jessica Louisa Maud Sweetapple, to go out into the world and fight such evil as she may find there.'

Gently, Sir Lancelot placed the chain over her head. She felt a shudder pass through her body as the crystal touched her hair. Sir Lancelot lifted her hair from beneath the chain and let it fall back down over it. Jessica took the crystal apple in her hand and as she did so she felt its power and protection. With this apple she felt safe. With this apple she could conquer Miss Darknight.

'It will keep you in touch with the Ancestors, Jessica. But remember this: it's not magic; it can't perform miracles.' Sir Lancelot rested his hand gently on her head.

She gazed out into the crowd and saw how greatly the Ancestors wished her well. She looked into the faces of her dearest Ancestors: Grandma and Grandpa Liddell and Great-Uncle Nelson Sweetapple. She would fight this battle for their sakes, and for her mother and father.

Jessica realised now that it wasn't just Miss Darknight versus Jessica Sweetapple, but Miss Darknight versus the whole Sweetapple dynasty, past, present and future. It was time to stop thinking only of herself and think of that; she was one small person measured against the whole sweep of family history.

The thought that everyone was depending on her ought to have been a frightening one, but instead it gave her courage. 'This is my destiny,' she murmured to herself. And now she knew for certain that this was true. 'I am the Special Child.' There was no one else, no first reserve or understudy: it was all up to her; to her and to her father, who was roaming the great wide world in his search for the perfect wood.

She followed Sir Lancelot and Lady Imogen down the steps and into the main body of the cave. Ancestors thronged around them, congratulating her, wishing her well, hugging her; it was almost impossible to move.

'Make way! Make way!' called the bugler boy. 'Let the Special Child pass.'

Almost before Jessica knew what was happening she felt herself being swept out of the cave. And she hadn't said goodbye to Grandma Liddell. Frantically she turned to wave but her favourite Ancestors were lost in the crowd.

'Sir Lancelot, please! I have to say goodbye to Grandma Liddell. Please!'

Sir Lancelot whispered something to the bugler boy and within seconds the bugle sounded. 'Make way for Grandma and Grandpa Liddell! Make way for Great-Uncle Nelson Sweetapple.'

As if by magic, the crowd parted and she saw her three best Ancestors. She ran towards them and hugged them in turn. She clung to Grandma Liddell as if she never wanted to let her go. Grandma took Jessica's face in both hands and kissed her soundly. 'Good luck, Special Child.'

Sir Lancelot cleared his throat and Lady Imogen took her elbow. 'Time to go,' she said.

'Come with me as far as the door, Grandma.'

Grandma nodded. 'We will.'

Now Jessica found herself at the head of a

procession that trailed across the seabed in a great winding throng. But this time it was heading for the door of the galleon.

When they reached it she turned and hugged Sir Lancelot and Lady Imogen. 'I'll do my best for you,' she promised.

Lady Imogen kissed her. 'I know you will, my dear.'

Sir Lancelot coughed and looked embarrassed all of a sudden. He kissed her quickly so that his nose banged against her cheek in an undignified collision.

She threw her arms round Grandma and Grandpa Liddell. 'And I'll do my best for you, too.'

All too soon the door was open and Jessica looked inside at the sea-empty interior. She could smell sawdust and tar. Quickly she stepped inside and waved. The sea blurred and she found it difficult to see those left behind.

Great-Uncle Nelson was to accompany her as far as the door into her bedroom. He closed the door between galleon and sea, quickly and firmly. Without looking at her, he strode towards the upper decks. 'Best get going,' he called quickly.

They climbed up through the decks until they reached fresh blue air. Jessica sniffed at its salty tang. Great-Uncle Nelson gave her one of his enormous bear hugs and she lifted her hand to his lovely red face and his hair as white as clouds. 'Goodbye, Uncle,' she said. Then she turned away from him.

Her heart thumped with a fierce sort of joy that left her breathless. She was to lead the Sweetapples into battle; a battle without swords or guns or bombs; a battle where the only ammunition would be good versus evil.

A great ship plunged through the wall
of Jessica Sweetapple's bedroom.
Not a whole ship; just the front part,
the prow. It was as high as the ceiling
and as wide as the wall. The room was
full of ship. But now the figurehead
of the great ship lay on the floor.
Life drained from it. Its wooden fingers
had uncurled. Soon the wooden apple
would fall from its feeble grasp,
and roll across the decaying wood
of the dying floor.

Part Two

Into
Battle

11. Prisoner!

Jessica stepped through the door of the galleon and back into her room. Instantly she felt the house's silence. She crossed the floor of her bedroom and stepped out on to the galleried landing.

Something was wrong. The silence was greater here, as if even the echoes of the past had been stifled.

'Mother!' The sound of her voice bounced back at her. Silence.

She glanced round, her eyes taking in everything. The gallery edged all four sides of the Great Hall with its gleaming dark wood. On the fourth side, the great oak staircase, wide as a bus, swept up from the black and white tiles of the hall floor. Suits of armour stood at ordered intervals round the landing, and portraits of the Ancestors hung against the honey stone of the walls.

She looked at the Family Tree, then reached out through the twisted curls of the bannister rails and touched the topmost branches. She pulled her hand away. The bare winter wood was soft and black, oozing, sticky as liquorice. Its leaves withered on the branch. The Family Tree was dying.

She gasped and pulled her hand away. 'Mother! Mother!' She leaped to her feet and ran along the landing, her breath tight in her chest. But when she reached the top of the stairs she stopped. Stopped fast.

The walls were bending, curling inwards towards her. The latticed windows were misted over like sightless eyes. The house was dying and Jessica felt helpless. If she had ever, for one minute, thought that she was the Special Child, she knew now that she was not.

She sat down at the top of the stairs, leaning forward, her arms hugging her knees and her head on her lap, wishing it were Grandma Liddell's lap instead. How had she ever let them talk her into believing she was the Special Child? Why had she been persuaded by them, when she alone knew what a coward she was? She would let them all down and let herself down too. What power did she have to change anything? None. She pinched the sides of her legs until it hurt too much and she had to stop. None!

She lifted her body slightly from her knees; something was pressing into her chest. She rubbed it and felt the cool round surface of the crystal apple. And it was as though she had touched the Ancestors; she felt their warmth and their certainty urging her on. 'When the time comes you will know what to do,' they had told her.

The crystal apple pulsed its streams of living water

through her body until she trembled with its sparkling energy. Its radiant blues and reds and greens zigzagged round the hallway, filling even the darkest, most hidden corner. Suddenly Jessica felt that she could climb Mount Everest, wrestle a lion, swim the channel – and still be back in time for tea. She danced down the stairs, pirouetting like a ballet dancer, lithe and strong as a jaguar. 'I am Jessica Louisa Maud Sweetapple. Special Child. Yes, I am!'

She danced out into the hall: invincible Jessica. And tripped full length on to the cold marble of the floor. Gasping with shock and pain, she pulled herself up into a sitting position. She rubbed at her elbows and shins.

'How could I be so stupid?'

Then she saw: the marble tiles were no longer smooth and flat on the floor's surface, but lay scattered in little mounds, as if molehills had erupted beneath them.

Cautiously she stood, took a few steps, then bent down again to examine the tiles. The earth was pushing itself up into the house. Small dirt mountains were heaving the tiles out of place. The earth was breaking in from below, destroying foundations and floors, and the air outside was pushing in so that the walls were bending and would eventually break.

Jessica had never felt so alone. Where was her mother?

Picking her way carefully across the broken floor, she headed towards the kitchen. The kitchen passage was long and dark with no windows. Normally it was lit by a single bulb high in the ceiling, but today it was not. She felt for the round brass switch on the wall to her right. She switched on the light.

A young girl stood at the end of the passage. Her smile sent ripples of cold along the narrow walkway and right into Jessica's face.

'Who are you?' Jessica whispered.

'My name's Lilith. What's that you're wearing?' She came nearer.

Jessica stepped backwards. Goose-pimples rose on her skin. Her legs weakened and shook. Her feet tripped over each other, awkward and clumsy, as if they were suddenly twice their usual size. She wanted to run but she couldn't.

The girl walked slowly down the passage. Suddenly she sprang forward and grabbed hold of Jessica's hair, winding it round her strong fist. Jessica felt her head tugged so sharply that she thought her neck might snap. The pain in her scalp caused tears to spring to her eyes. Pins and needles, like small electric shocks, pricked at her nose and seared into her head.

'Well now, what's this? Not tears? Surely the girl who's going to inherit Apple Manor isn't crying?' The girl laughed and tugged at Jessica's hair again.

'Let go!' Jessica kicked out at her captor, but the more she kicked, the more Lilith jumped and laughed.

'Let me go!' She pushed at the girl, but Lilith pinned both of Jessica's hands behind her back with her free hand. The other wound Jessica's long hair more firmly round her fist, so that the whole of its length was wound up almost to her neck.

'And what can this pretty bauble be?' She let go of Jessica's hands to grasp the crystal apple. Suddenly she screamed. 'It's hot! It's burning!' She wedged her hands between her knees to stop the fire.

Jessica turned to run but Lilith was too fast for her. She hadn't even reached the end of the passage before the girl had hold of her again.

Jessica fought like a wildcat but she was no match for Lilith.

'I'll get that apple from you, Jessica Sweetapple, don't you worry.'

Lilith pinned Jessica's arms behind her back once more, and this time she frogmarched her down the passage towards the kitchen. She kicked her from behind with each step she took. She used her forehead as a battering ram to open the kitchen door.

'Who are you? Why are you doing this to me?'

In the kitchen, Jessica could hardly see. Her eyes streamed with tears; not from crying, because she was determined *not* to cry in front of Lilith, but from pain. Her head throbbed with it, and her shoulders ached where the girl had pushed her hands further and further up her back.

Lilith pushed her roughly down and before she knew what was happening, another pair of hands had bound her tightly to a chair. She felt a cord winding itself round her body like a tight snake. It bit into her wrists and arms and her elbows pressed painfully into the chair back. But at least her hair was free at last.

She rubbed her head against her shoulder to wipe her eyes. When she looked up she saw her mother sitting exactly opposite her, bound in exactly the same way. Jessica could see right through her to the back of the chair.

'Darling. Thank goodness you're safe.' Carlotta Sweetapple smiled thinly and Jessica saw that her own presence was giving her mother strength. She watched her become more solid.

'Hello, Mother.' Jessica smiled.

Quick as a fly, something flicked at the side of her mother's chair. Miss Darknight, with a smile like tombstones, began to stroke Mrs Sweetapple's hair. 'Such beautiful hair. So soft. Silky as spiders' thread. What a pity you can't weave a web and capture me in it like a dark little fly.' Miss Darknight threw back her head and laughed so loudly that the echoes of it bounced against the walls, setting up shivers and chills along Jessica's spine.

'Now! We must have a conference. A *family* conference! We must sit one each side of the table to discuss matters. Lilith, you sit at the end.' Miss Darknight pointed to the far end of the table, underneath the great latticed windows that billowed and wept.

Lilith, who had been standing behind Jessica's chair, went to sit where she was told.

'What a good child,' said Miss Darknight. 'Child of my own. Lilith.'

'Your child?'

'My own, precious child, born of my body.' The woman smiled and blew a kiss at Lilith. 'My daughter.'

Daughter? Jessica struggled to imagine how such an evil woman could be a mother. Who was the father? She squirmed at the thought that they were part of her family.

'But the Ancestors never talked about you.'

'Of course not!' Miss Darknight snapped. 'They're ashamed of us.'

Jessica shivered. Miss Darknight *was* a ghost. She should have realised all along. And Lilith was one too. How stupid she'd been.

She shook so much with fear that her heels tapped against the chair legs. She wanted to cling to her mother but when she looked up she saw that her mother was transparent again.

Miss Darknight sat down at the head of the table. Behind her, mounted high up on the wall, hung a shield bearing the Sweetapple coat-of-arms.

Jessica was furious. 'How dare you sit there?' she shouted. 'You've got no right. It's my father's chair!'

Miss Darknight banged a small wooden hammer on the table. 'I call this meeting to order!'

'That's my hammer!' Jessica shouted. 'You took it from the nursery!'

'Darling. You know shouting gives me a headache.'

Miss Darknight reached the hammer and pegs across the table towards Jessica, then banged them even louder. She smiled. 'From the nursery. Yes.' She turned the hammer over and over in her hands, as though she'd never really looked at it before. 'For hammering round pegs into silly round wooden holes. I'm sure you'll miss it dreadfully.'

'Why don't you take the hammer if you like it so much? Take it and go. Take her.' Jessica glared at Lilith. 'Take your horrible cobwebs with you too. I'm going to save Apple Manor from your wickedness. Don't you know I'm the Special Child?'

'The *Special Child*?' Miss Darknight sneered down her long nose. Lilith laughed. 'The only Special Child round here is Lilith.'

Mrs Sweetapple looked quickly across at Jessica. 'Is it true, darling? Are you really the Special Child? How do you know?'

Jessica began to explain, enjoying telling the story in front of Miss Darknight and Lilith. It was right that they should know who she was and she felt a surge of pride as she described the empowering ceremony. She felt the crystal apple pulsating against her chest as she spoke, and her mother looked so proud that she almost became solid.

When Jessica had finished, Miss Darknight put down the hammer and smiled around the table. 'Lilith, why don't you make us all a nice cup of tea? I think we need it after listening to that display of nonsense. All with milk and no sugar. Thank you, dear.'

Lilith did as she was told, but kicked spitefully at Jessica's ankles as she passed her chair.

Miss Darknight unwound the cords that bound Mrs Sweetapple, then tied her hands together in front. She did the same with Jessica's cords.

'Now you'll be able to drink your tea. Aren't I kind?'

Jessica refused to drink hers when it came. Why was Miss Darknight humiliating them like this? Did it make her happy to see them frightened and squirming? She answered her own question: of course it did. She'd never seen the housekeeper so maniacally bright before. She was exhilarated by the power she had over them. She was having the time of her life – or death!

'I can see we're going to have to hold her nose, Lilith. Perhaps you could hold while I pour.'

'Really, Miss Darknight, please don't. She's just a child,' said Carlotta Sweetapple, horrified.

Lilith grasped Jessica's nose and used it as a handle to twist her head up. Jessica refused to open her mouth until lack of breath gave her no choice. She gulped a great breath of air and Miss Darknight put the cup to her mouth and tipped it violently. Jessica spat the tea squarely and wetly into Miss Darknight's bosom. It spattered so far that it even wet the cobwebs on the brooch.

'Oops a daisy,' she said gleefully. If she was going to be treated like a baby she may as well act like one.

Miss Darknight slammed the cup on to the table, then went to the sink where she dabbed herself with a tea-towel.

'Now then, ladies, after that silly behaviour, let me outline my plan for you. I'm sure you'll agree that it makes perfect sense. Apple Manor is dying, as you see. When I was denied my rightful inheritance, I vowed that I would move heaven and earth to get what belonged to me. If I couldn't do that, then I would destroy the place.'

'The eldest child inherits,' said Mrs Sweetapple reasonably. 'You were Nelson's younger sister, therefore Nelson inherited.'

'You can't split a house in two,' said Jessica. 'Great-Uncle Nelson offered to let you share.'

'I don't want to *share*. I want it all for myself. My brother Nelson had no children; by rights, Apple Manor should have come to me when he died. But instead he left it to your line of Sweetapples. And it was mine!'

Suddenly Miss Darknight's voice took on a deep, spiteful note. 'I shall have Apple Manor for myself, and for my daughter Lilith, not you: you will die!'

Jessica stared at Lilith's face. The girl's strong hands, wrapped round her cup, were white as lard. She smiled adoringly at Miss Darknight.

Adoringly? Jessica studied the girl's face. Love glowed from her eyes; travelled all the way to Miss Darknight's face, to her eyes. How could *anyone* love Miss Darknight?

She suddenly remembered what Great-Uncle Nelson had said about his sister, that things had gone wrong for her so that she grew bitter and angry, but that she did have some good deeds recorded in the treasure chest. She couldn't be *all* bad. Jessica remembered something else.

'What is it you've come to find?' she asked.

Lilith and Miss Darknight looked at one another. Flickers of alarm passed across their faces but neither of them answered her question.

'That got you, didn't it? You're scared. What are you scared of?' If she could find out, it might help her to save Apple Manor.

Now Jessica spoke very quietly. 'What are you looking for, Euphemia Darknight? Tell me.'

The big kitchen almost rang with silence. Lilith looked fearfully at her mother, whose face was even whiter than usual. Mrs Sweetapple glanced anxiously at Jessica.

Miss Darknight banged the wooden hammer and shattered the silence. 'Back to business! I shall destroy *you*. *You*, Carlotta Sweetapple. *You*, Jessica Sweetapple. And if he ever comes back from his ridiculous attempt to find suitable wood for the figurehead, I shall kill your father. The Sweetapples will be wiped out. Then Lilith and myself can live here for ever.'

With identical gestures, both Lilith and Miss Darknight clapped their hands together and laughed.

'You seem to have forgotten something,' said Jessica defiantly. 'If my father doesn't come back, then Apple Manor's going to die anyway. The house can't survive without a new figurehead, and only my father can make it.'

'Stuff and nonsense! Lilith and I will come up with something suitable. We'll find a decent carpenter who'll carve a likeness of Lilith and myself; something simple and elegant. That's after you've all been killed, of course: first things first.'

'What are you going to do to us?' Jessica asked.

'Well, my dear, bearing in mind the nautical history of the Sweetapples, Lilith and I have devised the most amusing plan. You're going to walk the plank.'

12. The smoking-trough

'I think we should untie them for a moment, don't you, Lilith?' Miss Darknight spoke sweetly, as if proposing a strawberry tea.

Lilith tugged spitefully at Jessica's cords, causing them to dig deeper. 'They'll be even tighter next time,' she hissed. 'But never mind, you won't have to put up with them for long. Once you hit that water, that'll be the end of you.'

The water in the moat was deep. In fact, legend said that it was bottomless. Jessica swallowed hard. How long would it take to die?

'There now! All untied. Wiggle your hands, Carlotta. Get the circulation moving.' Miss Darknight spoke as though she craved nothing more than Mrs Sweetapple's best welfare.

'Now, ladies. What a surprise I have for you! Come over here and look.'

Miss Darknight stood beneath the great latticed windows. She opened out the lowest pair and breathed in deeply. Then she wiped the snow from the windowledge and leaned out. She looked up towards the sky. 'Come on, ladies; it's the most beautiful sight!'

Jessica and her mother stood up from the table at the same time; at opposite sides, they reached the end of it together. Mrs Sweetapple stretched out her hand to her daughter. Jessica took it and squeezed hard; she felt strength flow through her and when she turned to look at her mother, she too seemed stronger; she was almost solid. Hand in hand they walked to the window.

Cold whipped at Jessica's cheeks as she craned her

neck to look skyward out of the casement which was high; she had to stand close to the wall in order to look upwards. At first she couldn't understand what it was she was seeing. But then, as understanding came, her heart froze as cold as the snow.

Jutting out from the balcony, outside her own bedroom window, was a thin wooden plank. She was looking at the underneath of it. It was only wide enough to take two feet. It would be a terrifying, dizzying fall into the moat below.

'Being a woman of compassion, I shall leave you two alone for your final hour; in any case, Lilith and I have last-minute preparations to complete. You will remain unbound. However, the door will be locked and there will be no way of escape. Make your peace with God now.'

Lilith followed her out, her face masked with smug satisfaction. As she left the kitchen she turned and gave a mock curtsey. 'Goodbye, Special Child. *And* her mother.'

The door banged and the key turned firmly in its lock.

The great brass clock ticked against the wall. The coals in the fire sputtered. Jessica sighed. Mrs Sweetapple wept silently, her hand clasped round her daughter's hand.

'There's no escape,' she sobbed.

Jessica didn't hear. In her mind she covered every centimetre of the room. All along one wall, pine cupboards reached to the ceiling. On another hung copper pans and dishes. On another, a row of bells for the servants who worked at Apple Manor in years gone by.

On the fourth wall were the two fireplaces. One was the black lead range where a fire burned, heating the ovens at its side and the kettle or saucepans above. Next to this was a huge inglenook fireplace, containing a spit big enough to roast a whole sheep. They lit this fire only at Christmas and other celebrations.

Jessica slipped her hand away from her mother's. 'What an idiot I am! Look, Mother, if I fetch the steps from the alcove, I'll be able to reach the catch and open the window. And then I can find something to put on top of the steps so that I can climb out!'

Mrs Sweetapple lifted her head and brushed away her tears. 'You can stand on my shoulders! You're not very heavy.'

Jessica smiled and kissed her mother on the forehead. She used her sleeve to wipe away the last of the tears and Mrs Sweetapple caught hold of her hand. 'You're a good, brave girl, Jessica, and I'm so sorry I've been like this. I don't know what's been happening to me.'

Swiftly there came into her mind an image of her mother, chasing down the drive of Apple Manor. She was after a man she'd caught trying to break into the house, and she was strong and fearless. She hadn't caught him but he'd never come back again. Mr Sweetapple had laughed and called her 'Carlotta the Canonball'.

'Do you remember the burglar?' Jessica asked.

Her mother smiled. 'That was the old me,' she said.

'Well, the old you must still be in there somewhere, Mother.'

'I think Miss Darknight stole her,' she whispered.

'I'm terrified Miss Darknight's going to make me walk the plank,' said Jessica.

'Then you'd better go and fetch those steps from the alcove.' Her mother pushed her gently forward. 'Go on.'

When she returned, Mrs Sweetapple opened the steps for her and held them steady while she climbed.

'It won't open!' Jessica stood back from the window, almost in despair. It had seemed such a simple thing to do, when she'd thought of it.

'The windows lock automatically when you close them. You need a key. I'd forgotten.' Mrs Sweetapple dragged herself back to the table and collapsed on to a chair. 'I'd forgotten.'

'Well where is it?' But Jessica knew the answer, even as she asked.

'Where do you think? Who has control of everything in this house now?' Her mother's voice was barely a whisper. She put her head on her arms as though she was going to sleep.

Jessica jumped from the steps and ran to her

mother. She shook her shoulder roughly. 'Remember who you really are, Mother! Miss Darknight *has* got control now but we're going to stop her. This isn't the real you. Where are you?'

But Mrs Sweetapple didn't respond.

'Oh, what's the use. She's cast some sort of spell on you and you're just hopeless!' Would she even have the strength to go with Jessica? What would happen to her mother if she was left behind? What would Miss Darknight do to her?

A sob caught in Jessica's throat and she ran desperately round the room, looking for an escape route. She felt wild, out of control, she had to keep moving.

Then she stopped herself. This was getting them nowhere; she must calm down and think.

Slowly she forced herself to pace the kitchen's perimeter. She tried the door but it was locked, as she'd known it would be. She pulled open every cupboard door, in case by some miracle there was a hidden way out of the kitchen: a secret passage.

'This is stupid! There are no secret passages.'

Finally she looked at the two fireplaces. There was a red-hot fire in one, but maybe there was somewhere they could hide in the inglenook. She walked towards it slowly. There were two old bread ovens in the brick walls at either side. Only a small child could have hidden there.

Above the inglenook lay a stone smoking-trough where, in years gone by, whole pigs would be smoked for bacon and ham. She remembered her father holding her aloft so that she could see inside. She remembered stories of chimney-sweeps from olden days, and how much room there was for Santa Claus. She knew that it was possible to climb into the trough from the front of the inglenook, and then up the chimney to the roof.

'Mother, I've got an idea. Look! Come over here!'

But her mother had almost faded away again. Jessica ran across to her and pulled her folded arms from under her head. 'Don't go away now, please!' She stroked her mother's soft hair. 'Please be strong for me. Try!'

Mrs Sweetapple slowly lifted her head, as if it was

almost too heavy for her neck to support. 'I'll do my best, my dear.' Her voice was husky, hardly even a whisper; she faded to a mist as she spoke. She had withdrawn to that secret place where no one could follow.

Quickly, Jessica fetched the wooden steps from under the windows. In a few seconds she was at the level of the smoking-trough; a few seconds more and she was crouching inside. It was dark and smelled of old smoke and soot. When she looked upwards, she saw that the entrance to the chimney was blocked by a wooden trapdoor. She pushed with all her strength, but the trapdoor moved not a millimetre. She sat down at the base of the trough.

'I can't do it! I can't!' All her energy slipped away and gradually her eyes began to close. Jessica curled herself into a ball like a small animal and drifted off to sleep.

She was cold. A mournful noise filled the whole of the small cramped space. She knew that it was the sound of her own sobbing; sobbing that came because she had given up, had decided that it would be better to starve to death in that airless, cramped place than it would be to walk the plank. She would simply wait to die.

She blinked her eyes as something flashed brightly. She looked downwards. It was the crystal apple, pulsing against her chest like a crystal heart. She picked it up and held it close to her face. Lights sprang from end to end of the trough like colourful bursts of electricity, and deep inside, deeper than the apple could possibly be, she saw the faces of Sir Lancelot and Lady Imogen. She knew with absolute certainty that they did *not* want her to die. In fact, from the expression on their faces, she felt they were *commanding* her not to die.

Their faces faded and the lights in the trough went back into the crystal. Now there were just steady pulses of light contained within the beads and the apple itself. Jessica sighed. There was work to be done.

Slowly she uncurled her cramped limbs and stretched her arms. Her hand hit something cold and metallic. Her fingers probed, trying to discover what it was. It didn't take her long to realise that it was a key, suspended from a hook in the brickwork.

It was huge. It was heavy and black. She lifted it from the hook and held it in both hands. Why would there be a key tucked away right here? Slowly her frozen thoughts began to thaw. To unlock a trapdoor perhaps? She looked up to find that the trapdoor did indeed have a very large keyhole.

'Yes! Yes!'

The trapdoor was made of solid wood, hinged to open downwards. She wasn't all that strong; she might get crushed by the thing. Too bad: what other option was there? She put the key in the lock and found that it turned smoothly.

The trapdoor was heavy, but Jessica was just able to support its weight as she carefully lowered it. As the trapdoor approached the side wall of the smoking-trough, she had barely enough room to squeeze round the edge of it and avoid being trapped, and as she let it bang against the wall she felt the accumulated debris of years raining down on her. She found herself covered with soot, twigs and fragments of blackened brick. She coughed and choked and spluttered.

'Mother! Where are you?' Jessica tried to rub the soot out of her eyes, but she seemed only to rub it in. 'Mother?' She scrambled awkwardly down from the smoking-trough to find her mother waiting at the bottom for her.

'My goodness, Jessica; you're going to take some cleaning up.'

'We're about to walk the plank and all you can do is complain that I'm dirty!' But Mrs Sweetapple's remark made her look down at her soot-blackened clothes. Almost against her will, she tried to imagine how they would ever come clean again. 'I'll have to jump in the moat!' she said. And then suddenly she began to laugh. She clung to her mother and before long they were both laughing helplessly.

When they finally stopped, Mrs Sweetapple gave Jessica a hug. 'Good luck, Jessie. Everyone's relying on you.'

'You mean the Ancestors?'

Her mother nodded. 'I've found it difficult to

remember them since Miss Darknight came. I kept trying to hang on to the memory of the stories your father told me about them, but they just seemed to fade away like a dream in the morning.'

Jessica held her mother tight and wished more than anything that she could come too. But she couldn't. All Jessica could now do was pray that she would be safe. And save Apple Manor for her mother's sake.

13. On the roof

Jessica was at the bottom of the chimney, and when she looked upwards she could see daylight. It was a long, long way to climb. One slip and she would fall. She breathed deeply. It was no good worrying about that. If this didn't work, she was going to fall anyway. She noticed the brick footholds jutting out from the chimney sides, put there for the chimney-sweep boys. With hands and feet struggling to catch hold of the jutting bricks, Jessica climbed. As the chimney rose higher it grew narrower. Her boots scraped against the rough wall, then her foot caught in the folds of her skirt. She scraped her knuckles painfully against the brickwork as she pulled the material free. She dared not think about the yawning black space beneath her.

She reached for the next handhold and nudged against something hard. She pulled herself upwards and saw that this handhold was a narrow ledge. Placed right in the middle of it was a small wooden box. She felt the crystal apple pulsing excitedly. Sparks of silver light showered the box, urging her to take it. She pulled it towards her and lifted the lid. It contained what seemed to be letters and something shiny that rattled, but it was too dark to see properly. Whoever had put the box there certainly hadn't intended it to be found. There was no way she'd be able to carry it; she needed both hands to keep herself from falling. With one hand she unfastened the top four buttons of her blouse, then, very carefully, she lifted the box and slid it inside. It dropped down towards the waistband of her skirt and lodged there.

She was only a metre or so below the chimney opening when she realised that it was covered with chicken wire, to stop birds falling down and becoming trapped.

Jessica panicked. Her palms were sweating so that she thought she would lose her grip and fall. The breath came tight in her chest and she wheezed noisily. Dizziness wrapped its coils round her and threatened to push her away from the side of the chimney: down, down, down.

'Stop it!' She spoke to herself sternly. Her voice echoed and bounced up and down the chimney's length. She willed herself to breathe deeply. One at a time she took her hands away from the brick hold and wiped them down the sides of her skirt. Then she began to climb again.

When she reached the top she found, to her relief, that the chicken wire had not been secured to the chimney stack. She easily pushed it off. She put her hands over the sides of the stack and heaved herself upwards. But the box made her too big to get through the narrow opening. She sighed. 'Come on, Jessica, you can do it.'

Carefully, with one elbow held firmly over the edge of the chimney stack and her feet pressed hard against the walls, she pulled the box from out of her blouse and dropped it over the edge. It clattered down on to the roof.

One more push found her almost halfway out. Another push and she was sitting on the edge of the chimney with her feet dangling down the side of the stack. The roof sloped gently down to a wide parapet. Jessica knew that it was possible to walk on its wide ledge all the way round the roof of Apple Manor.

She sat for a while, thinking what to do. She could find her way to the ground and just run away, out of the village. But that wouldn't do any good. Miss Darknight and Lilith would have won. They would own Apple Manor. And she couldn't leave her mother to walk the plank.

The plank! Jessica clutched at the chimney in

excitement. If she sabotaged the plank, nobody could walk it! 'Brilliant, Jessica!'

She looked at the snow-covered roof. Then, with one hand on the chimney stack, she wrapped her skirt tightly round her legs and sat at the top of the slope. She closed her eyes and let go. She felt the cold wind on her face and heard the hiss of snow as it rushed beneath her. She bumped on to the parapet and opened her eyes.

The parapet was edged by a fine stone balustrade, with each separate spindle shaped out of twelve stone apples, piled one above the other. She looked through the gaps at the view of the snow-covered countryside. Up the lane she could see the schoolhouse and felt a pang of sadness for her lost friends. She wondered where Lauren and Guy were; what Thomas and Oliver were doing. Were they missing her, too?

She sighed and leaned over the balustrade to look down the side of the house. She saw that she was directly above her own bedroom window, with the dreadful plank jutting out from her balcony. There was only one way down. She must use the sturdy old branches of the ivy. From there she might be able to get back into her bedroom and the safety of the ship.

She felt the crystal apple buzzing and humming at her chest. Blue and gold lights streamed from it in long, pulsating tendrils. She turned and saw the box. It had come to rest about ten metres away, on the stone walkway. The lights from the apple linked her to it and she followed them across the roof.

When Jessica lifted its lid she found five things inside the box. Right at the top was a letter. She opened it out and began to read.

The Old Shipping House
Portsmouth Quay

Dear Mrs Pottage,
*   It is my painful duty to confirm that SS Midnight has been lost, with all hands on board. As you know, the ship had been missing for some time but as communication between the New World and England is notoriously bad, we had been unable to establish what had happened to her.*

*Some weeks ago, the box which you will find enclosed
was washed ashore, along with some personal effects
belonging to other members of the crew. Please be so
kind as to let us know that you have received the box
and its contents safely.*

With my condolences,

Admiral Jeremiah Booth

At the bottom of the box lay two rolls of heavy white
paper, browning with age and stained with the marks
of salt water. Both of them were tied with pink
ribbon. On top of these lay a ring in a blue velvet box,
and an oval silver locket the size of an egg.

It took a while for her cold, stiff fingers to prise
the locket open, but when she did, Jessica found
herself looking at a younger Miss Darknight. Facing
her was a heavily bewhiskered man with a too-red
face and piercing blue eyes. In writing as fine as a
spider's leg, the artist had written: Captain Silas
Pottage and his wife, Euphemia.

A sudden gust of wind made Jessica shiver. She
looked out across the snow-trapped fields and into

the distance. Miss Darknight had a husband: Captain Pottage, the man she'd imagined talking to when Jessica had watched her through the telescope. At some time in her life, before Lilith, Miss Darknight had loved someone, and someone had loved her.

Now Jessica picked up the ring. It was made of a series of gold apples linked together. 'How dare she use the emblem of Apple Manor!'

Jessica dropped the ring back into the box and sighed. Uncle Nelson's voice echoed in her memory. Once, before any of this had happened, before Father left, she remembered him saying: 'You must take the rough with the smooth, Jess; the good with the bad; it's all part of life's pattern and everything has its place. How would you know morning had come if there had been no night? How could we be joyful when spring arrived if there'd been no winter?'

She looked out across the fields again. Miss Darknight's arrival had brought everlasting winter; the snow had lain on the ground for months and months now. She remembered Miss Darknight's good deeds, recorded in the treasure chest by Uncle Nelson. 'How does it all fit together?' she murmured to herself.

And what about Lilith, who was spiteful and malicious? Until the housekeeper had come, Jessica had known only kindness, but who had been kind to Lilith? Miss Darknight was kind to her, yes, she'd seen that with her own eyes; but some time in her life Lilith had been angry and sad and she couldn't get rid of those feelings. Had she caught them from her mother?

Jessica slipped the locket and ring into her deep pocket, then picked up one of the scrolls of paper. Quickly she untied the ribbon and opened it out. It was a sort of birth certificate.

> *To Captain Silas Britannica Pottage and his wife Euphemia, a daughter, Lilith Christina. The bells of Apple Manor ring in joyful celebration and are echoed in heaven. May God bless the child, Lilith Christina, and her devoted parents. May she bring honour to her family.*

Jessica felt somehow subdued and sad; not for herself but for Lilith and Miss Darknight. 'You're going soft, Jessica Sweetapple,' she whispered to herself. 'Feeling sorry for people who are trying to kill you.'

Quickly she opened out the second scroll. But there were pages of it, all in tiny handwriting; there was no time to read it now. She pushed it deep into her pocket, where it crackled uncomfortably against the side of her leg. Then she put the box back on the roof. She'd be able to collect it some other time, if she survived.

She began to climb over the edge of the parapet.

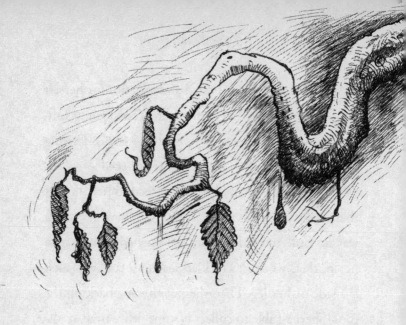

14. Perilous journey

*C*limbing over the edge of the parapet was even more scary than scaling the chimney. Jessica stepped out into empty space until she stood on the outside of the balustrade, with the walls of the house falling away beneath her. She wedged her feet firmly between the stone spindles and clutched tightly at the rail.

Jessica looked down. The distant gardens shimmered and danced as her vision blurred. Her head swam and her palms ran with sweat. She was sure she would fall into the moat. She gripped the spindles more tightly as she felt the strength draining from her hands. Her legs shook so much that she knew at any moment her feet would slip. Her ears filled with a rushing noise and she could hardly breathe; her chest felt as though a tight band pressed round it. She threw herself back across the balustrade to land painfully on the stone parapet.

Slowly her breathing returned to normal; the cold of the melting snow against her face made her sit up. She hadn't escaped anything. She had no alternative but to climb back over that balustrade and down the ivy to her bedroom. Jessica acted quickly and forced herself not to think of falling. Before she'd had time to wonder how she'd got there, she found herself clinging to the walls of the house like a monkey. She swallowed and rested her head for a moment against the branches of the ivy. 'Come on, Jessica Sweetapple. Don't give up now! What would Father think if he knew you'd given up?' She thought of his patient work, carving beautiful things. Sometimes he couldn't make his hands do what his heart and imagination told them. Then he would start all over again, until his hands and his heart and his mind began to work together. He never gave up.

She gave a deep sigh. She lowered first one foot, then the other. The ivy held firm. At every movement she tested its strength. And with a hand and a foot, and a hand and a foot, she descended the wall until at last she was able to place her feet on the ledge of her bedroom balcony. She took a deep breath, then jumped.

She landed right outside her bedroom window. She stood up and rubbed the snow from her hands and knees. Her hands were now so numb with cold that she hardly felt the grazes. She turned to examine the plank.

It had been lashed to the top of the balcony with thin rope. It shouldn't be too difficult to untie it and toss the plank over the edge and into the moat. At least it would delay things if Miss Darknight had to look for another one.

She reached out and pressed down on the plank,

then let go. It sprang up and down several times, and that was when the pressure had been exerted from the anchored end. If she were to stand on it, it would bend downwards and she would slide off into the moat. She had imagined, from pirate stories she had read, that you would be able to walk to the end and then jump off in your own good time. Not with this plank, you wouldn't.

She turned to her bedroom and saw, with a pang of both longing and relief, the prow of the ship. She reached eagerly for the window before realising that there was no handle on the outside. The windows were firmly closed against the cold and even if she somehow managed to smash the thick glass, the criss-cross metal latticing would prevent her from getting through.

'I'm not going to walk the plank after all. I'm going to freeze to death instead!' She tucked her icy fingers beneath her arms to try to get some warmth into them. She closed her hand round the crystal apple, and felt again that curious, comforting sensation of being in touch with the Ancestors.

'Where are you, Grandma Liddell? Can you see me? Do you know what's happening to me?'

She lifted the crystal apple and watched the beautiful lights dancing inside; streams of radiant pink and blue and green. 'Fat lot of good you've been so far,' she informed it crossly. 'It's no good just looking pretty, you ought to *do* something.' She banged it against the window furiously. To her amazement, a crack spread like lightning across the glass.

Then she noticed the curling snail shape of the window's handle.

'Jessica Sweetapple, you are so stupid sometimes!' All she had to do was break the glass near the handle, put her hand through and open the window from the inside. She took the crystal apple from round her neck and kissed it. 'I'm sorry I was rude to you.'

Suddenly the faces of all her best Ancestors appeared again inside the apple. Grandma Liddell smiled and waved, Lady Imogen and Sir Lancelot stood tall and regal, whilst Great-Uncle Nelson danced the Sailor's Hornpipe and sucked at a strawberry ice-lolly; he'd obviously spent Sir Lancelot's groat! Jessica smiled and waved to them.

'Can you see me? Can you?'

But as she watched, the Ancestors disappeared. The beautiful lights darted once more inside the crystal and she knew that she must act quickly.

She pulled her hand back as far as it would go. 'I hope this isn't going to break you,' she whispered to the crystal. Then with all her strength she smashed it against the glass. A fine network of cracks spread across the window. But it didn't break.

'Try again,' she muttered to herself.

This time she used less strength but aimed her blow more accurately. At the first sharp tap, the glass splintered near the handle. She chipped away at it until she felt the glass give beneath her hand. A few more careful taps and she had widened the hole enough to reach in and turn the handle. It lifted easily and she pulled the window towards her. She slipped the crystal beads back round her neck then, stiff with cold, she climbed on to the windowledge inside, and jumped down on to the floor of her beloved bedroom. She tiptoed across the room to lock her bedroom door.

She leaned against the prow of the galleon and breathed a huge sigh of relief. Whatever happened next, at least she was safe for the time being. She needed to see Grandma Liddell before there were any more battles to be fought; needed to sit on her knee in the rocking-horse and be lulled by her soothing voice.

She was startled by a creaking noise. The door of her wardrobe swung slowly open. Inside the dark space, with only their white faces showing in the gloom, stood Lilith and Miss Darknight.

15. An old, old story

They sprang towards her.

Jessica stepped back. One foot stumbled over the other and she pivoted, bottom first, on to the wooden floor. They had hold of her before she could think. They dragged her up and threw her across the bed. Miss Darknight pinned her arms down whilst Lilith bound both wrists tight.

Jessica swung her body round and lashed out with

her feet, making contact with Miss Darknight's leg. But the woman's long skirts muffled the attack and she leaped nimbly out of the way.

Jessica struggled and kicked and fought. 'Why are you doing this to me?' She felt tears not far away but was determined that Miss Darknight wouldn't see. She was even more determined that Lilith wouldn't.

'Because you're the Special Child, stupid. And because we hate you.' Lilith's voice was a syrupy sneer.

'Shut up, Lilith! Close the door! Can't you hear them?'

All three of them listened. Jessica lifted her head. The door to the ship was still open. She could hear the voices of the Ancestors calling. 'Euphemia! Euphemia! Come back!'

'Why don't you go to the ship, where you belong? They're calling for you!'

'Because they choose to be good and follow the cycle of life and death. But I don't want to be good, I want revenge. I want what's mine.'

'It's not yours!' Jessica shouted. 'You know it's not!'

'Euphemia! Euphemia!' The voices of the Ancestors seemed closer.

'Great-Uncle Nelson, help me! Sir Lancelot!'

'Shut the door, Lilith. Shut it! Be quick!'

The voice of Euphemia Darknight trembled. Her grip on Jessica's legs loosened. Jessica sat up and swung her legs over the side of the bed. She ran to the door of the ship but Lilith barred her way. She tried to push her to one side but her hands were tied and the girl was too strong.

'Grandma Liddell, help me! Great-Uncle Nelson! Please!'

But the door was firmly closed and there was no way through. She knew that there was no point in trying to fight Lilith and Miss Darknight, not physically anyway: they were both too strong for her. Her only chance was to trick them. She returned to the bed and sat down. She had no tricks.

Miss Darknight stood by the bed, trembling. She stared at the door of the ship as if she thought it might suddenly open. Jessica had seen the woman afraid before, but now she seemed terrified.

There was silence in the room and Jessica longed to break it.

'We must go and fetch the woman, Lilith. We must bring Carlotta here. But first we have to make sure that *she* doesn't escape.'

Jessica was made to sit down, and then Miss Darknight secured her arms by binding them tightly with cord wrapped round the chair. At the door she turned and looked at Jessica with cold, glittering eyes. 'There is no escape, Jessica Sweetapple.'

In the silence after they had left, Jessica's gaze travelled upwards to the scar where the figurehead had been. The wood looked naked there; it looked sore, like a wound that wouldn't heal. Sap dripped into a little puddle on the floor. But the dripping was slowing down, the life in the wood was drying out.

'Father's return won't make any difference now,' she whispered. 'It will be too late. When he gets here we'll be dead at the bottom of the bottomless moat.'

She tried to picture her father's face but it had faded from her memory, just like her mother had faded. Jessica turned to look at the photograph of him beside her bed, and her father's smiling face flooded back into her heart. She longed for him.

'A weakling. A no-good wood-carver,' Miss Darknight had called him. And there had been a smile on her thin, cold lips. He wasn't a weakling. He was going to carve a new figurehead and save Apple Manor. But where was he? Why didn't he come?

Jessica fidgeted on the hard wooden chair and heard a crackling noise. The last letter! She had almost forgotten about it.

Because her hands were tied at the front, she was able to pull the folds of her skirt round so that she could just about reach into her pocket. She opened the letter and began to read.

Apple Manor

To My Dear Husband, Silas,
Although it is many years since you have answered our letters, and many more since we last saw you, today I must write and tell you my dreadful news.

This morning, after five days of fever, our beloved child, Lilith, died. I do not know what I shall do.

During the time that her fever raged, she asked many times for you. 'Where is Papa? I want my papa.' Sometimes I felt that her sickened mind saw you clearly. 'Papa!' she shouted once. Her eyes were brighter even than the fever allowed, and for a few moments afterwards she seemed peaceful.

Of course she has no real memories of you. How could she? She was only an infant of a few months when you finally left us to sail for Botany Bay. I always told her that you would come back, even when I came to understand that you would never return; it seemed important to keep hope alive. However, she was doomed to die at the tender age of twelve years, without ever having that hope realised.

Tomorrow we will walk behind the black carriage to the church. There we shall thank God for Lilith's life and say our goodbyes to her.

If you receive this letter, even if you cannot answer it, please pray for us, for I do not know what I shall do now. It is many years since I received the letter from Admiral Booth, informing me that your ship was missing, but one small part of me still nurtures the hope that you are somewhere safe, trying to return to me and your child.

I shall send this letter to the Admiralty, urging them to renew and increase their efforts to find you, although in my heart of hearts I know that my hope is futile.

Your ever loving wife,

Euphemia Pottage

There were tears in Jessica's eyes as she rolled up the letter and put it back in her pocket. She thought of her father so far away, and how it must have been for Lilith never to have known her own father. And then to die without ever seeing him.

'Father.' She whispered his name, over and over. 'Father.' And then she was crying for him; deep, wracking sobs that she couldn't hold back. Her own father and Captain Pottage, Lilith and Jessica; it seemed that the whole world blurred and melted into one cry; a cry that was soon interrupted by the return of Miss Darknight with Lilith and Mrs Sweetapple.

Jessica tried to form a sentence in her head, about how she wished Miss Darknight and Lilith had lived happier lives; how she understood why they were so angry; how she wished Captain Pottage hadn't drowned at sea. But when had he died? Miss Darknight wrote to him about Lilith's death, hoping that he might still be alive, despite the letter from Admiral Booth.

She lifted her head to look at them all: at Lilith's hostile face and Miss Darknight's triumphant expression. Of Carlotta Sweetapple there was hardly anything left but an outline, and the dots of eyes, nose and mouth. The Ancestors were more real than her mother.

16. Seconds away from death

Miss Darknight turned to Mrs Sweetapple. 'Your daughter's been a very naughty girl. But we've had these problems with her before, haven't we, dear? Discipline never was your strong point, Carlotta. But never mind: punishment is at hand.'

Miss Darknight took all Jessica's sympathy and stamped on it until it was dead. Anger filled the gap that sympathy left; anger that felt bigger than Apple

Manor and all its history.

'I haven't done anything, you stupid old hag!'

'Old hag or not, my dear, in five minutes' time I'll be here and you'll be dead.'

'You're already dead, you're just pretending to be alive!'

Miss Darknight smiled.

Lilith giggled.

'But I'm really alive, and that's something you can never be again!'

'We'll see,' said Miss Darknight. 'Now, my dear, let's just unfasten those cords for you. I don't want you to have any problems climbing on to the plank. And they must be *so* uncomfortable.'

A few more minutes and Jessica would be in the ship for good, and she knew, with a sudden certainty, that she didn't want to be: not yet. She loved to see her Ancestors, she loved to visit them, but she loved to come back too, to Apple Manor and her friends. Her friends: where were they? What had happened to her father? She wanted to find them; she wasn't ready to die yet.

Miss Darknight unfastened the cords, then took her by the shoulders and turned her firmly round. 'On to the plank with you, Jessica. Chop chop.' She gave her an encouraging pat on the bottom. 'Just think how lucky you are, dear: eternity with those dreadful Ancestors of yours.'

'And yours! And Lilith's! It's no good trying to pretend they're not yours too.' Jessica's chin jutted defiantly. Even if she was going to die, she didn't have to do it quietly like a good little girl.

'I'll get you!' she glared. 'I've never hated anybody so much in my life! I don't know how I could ever have felt sorry for you and Lilith. I'd rather share Apple Manor with a snake! I'd rather touch a snake's fang than you!' She shrugged herself away from the woman's cold touch.

But Miss Darknight pushed her on to the window-ledge and out on to the balcony. Carlotta Sweetapple's sobs followed them.

'Come along, dear. I haven't got all day.' She put her hands round Jessica's waist and tried to lift her on to the plank.

'Get off me! I'll do it myself!' Jessica climbed backwards on to the plank and felt it give beneath her. She sat at the end, one hand still resting on the balustrade, facing the balcony.

'Turn round. How can you jump when you're facing the wrong way? Have some sense, dear. Turn round.' Miss Darknight tutted and flapped her hands.

Jessica saw that the stone of the balcony was crumbling. There was a dent where the plank bit into it, made worse by the weight of her body. The stone would not support the plank for much longer. There was very little time left for Apple Manor.

She looked out across the countryside to the farthest horizon where a farmhouse nestled within a cluster of trees. And it seemed as though she was viewing the world through the wrong end of a telescope: everything so far away, so small and distorted. The circle began to tilt from side to side like the swing of a pendulum, and Jessica felt her body sway with it: to and fro and to and fro and to and fro. It would be so easy just to let go and slip down into the dark clutches of the moat. Why was she still holding on? It was all so effortless, so easy, so simple, so beautiful.

'Hurry up, Jessica! Spread your arms out when you fall, like a bird. I want to see what happens when you hit the ice.' Lilith almost danced with excitement.

Jessica clutched at the plank. What was she thinking of? She'd been sent to save Apple Manor not to die. She was the Special Child! She shuffled towards the middle of the plank so that Miss Darknight wouldn't be able to reach her. She felt it dip – too far! She began to slide towards the end. Desperately she threw her body flat against the plank so that her full length lay along it, her arms and legs dangling over the side. Her head swam with dizziness as her eyes followed the walls of the house, down to the second floor windows, down to the first floor, down to the great entrance hall with its pillars and steps, down to the cellars, down to the moat. The walls seemed to teeter backwards and forwards as if they were about to lose their balance. Her arms and legs shook. She closed her eyes.

Snow, cold against her face, caused her to open them again. The flakes came thick and heavy, blurring the landscape as if a great fog had suddenly fallen. She pushed herself into a sitting position and looked back towards the balcony. 'If you want me to jump, you're going to have to come out and push me!'

Down through the swirling snow, Jessica suddenly saw a blur of colour: yellows, oranges, blues. Drifting upwards came the sound of children's voices. The snow came more thickly and the voices mingled with the rising wind.

> *My mother said*
> *I never should*
> *Play with the gypsies*
> *In the wood.*

Children! She felt a surge of hope that died immediately. She saw that these were the wooden children from school, not her friends from so long ago. The wind blew more fiercely now, whipping the snow into a frenzied blizzard. Jessica felt so alone, and so angry.

'No wonder Great-Uncle Nelson couldn't leave

Apple Manor to you!' she shouted. 'You're a horrible, wicked, evil person!'

'How dare you? How dare you speak to me like that? Jump off that plank this minute or I'll untie the rope.'

'Go on, then!'

'Think how undignified it would be – having to be thrown off; not even enough courage to jump!'

'Not even enough courage to face the Ancestors. That's you! You're just a cruel coward. I bet even your own mother didn't love you. I bet you had cobwebs all over you when you were born!'

'That's enough! You're going off that plank if it's the last thing I do!'

Jessica moved backwards, away from the woman. She felt something bulky against her leg. The letters!

'What about Captain Pottage? I've got his letters here. If you let me get off the plank, I'll show them to you. If not, they'll disappear into the moat with me.'

Miss Darknight looked at her daughter. The two of them seemed to freeze, like the snow.

'Papa?' Lilith's voice was faint. 'Has he come to the ship?'

'Not yet, my dear. The husband or wife of a Sweetapple is allowed on the ship only if their spouse is there too.'

'Why can't we go on the ship, then? Then he can come too. I want to see him.' Lilith laid her head against her mother's shoulder.

'I don't know where he is, Lilith,' Miss Darknight sighed.

Quietly, Jessica edged back towards the balcony.

'Get back!' Miss Darknight pointed at her as if she had a gun in her hand.

Jessica slid back a little.

'I've got his wedding ring too. And your portraits in the locket, and the letter that you sent to him and Lilith's birth certificate.' She was breathless; the wind was rising and snatching her breath. 'Did he die before he got your letters? He must have done, I'm sure. That's why he didn't reply.'

They were like statues now. They stared at her as if she were a ghost.

'Imagine how sad he must have been when he knew he was drowning, knowing that he'd never see you again.' Jessica was almost crying.

And then she noticed that *they* were crying; and then the most extraordinary thing of all: as the tears fell on to the brooch on Miss Darknight's dress, the cobwebs began to melt away and Jessica could see that it was attached to a silver chain. Jessica knew then that Miss Darknight had never cried before.

Perhaps it was the shock of her own crying that made Miss Darknight unfasten the clasp of the silver chain which, until now, had been hidden under the cobwebs and her collar. She let it fall. It slithered down the black silk of her blouse. She reached out her hand to catch it and fingered it gently. Then, with a great burst of anger, hurled it across the balcony. It hit the ground with a loud clink and the locket opened. There were two portraits inside. Jessica recognised the faces of Granny Hepzibah and her husband, Jonah Sweetapple: Euphemia Darknight's parents.

The sound of their cries rose from the locket as if

from a great distance. 'Euphemia! Lilith!' Their faces moved in sadness and the locket became filled with their tears.

Lilith and Miss Darknight gasped. Lilith put her hands to her face and Jessica saw that her eyes were wide with fear.

The crystal apple pulsed, and as soon as Jessica touched the surface she felt the warmth of its energy. The lights inside seemed more than usually agitated, so she closed her hand round it as if to capture the life of the apple within her own body. The voices of Hepzibah and Jonah Sweetapple soared into the air and blended with the wind.

Miss Darknight tiptoed slowly across the balcony. Gingerly, she lifted the locket from the floor and snapped it shut. As soon as their faces disappeared, the voices of the Ancestors were silenced. Lilith and Miss Darknight sighed, as though they had escaped from some malign power. And then Miss Darknight hurled the brooch out across the balcony. Jessica watched it curl out of sight, down into the moat.

'At last,' Miss Darknight murmured. 'After all these years, Lilith, we're rid of them. We're free.'

'Why didn't you do it sooner, then?' Lilith asked.

'You know I couldn't. You know it wouldn't come off.'

'Your tears melted the cobwebs, that's why,' said Jessica.

'What do you know? You're just an ignorant child!'

'Granny Hepzibah and Grandpa Jonah loved you.'

'You don't know what you're talking about!' Suddenly Miss Darknight lifted her head and howled like a banshee. The wind lifted its voice to howl with her. The noise went on and on and on; a frozen cry in a frozen landscape.

'I've got Captain Pottage's ring. Look.' Jessica held it out towards them. 'Did you give it to him? Was it his wedding ring?'

'Yes.' It was a whisper, snatched by the wind.

'Shall I come and give it to you? If I can get back on to the balcony I've got all his things here for you.'

'You stole them!' Miss Darknight's eyes glittered

dangerously, and Jessica knew that she had to be very, very careful.

'I found them in the chimney.'

'Snooping! You were snooping!'

'We wanted to look for his things! But you had to go and find them instead! I hate you, Jessica Sweetapple! He was *my* papa!' Lilith began to cry even harder and that started Miss Darknight off again.

'Well who put them up the chimney in the first place?' Jessica was puzzled; it seemed a strange thing to do.

'My father! News of my husband's death arrived the day after I buried our daughter. Father said he'd *disposed* of the box because I was pining over it. I had lost everything I loved. Stupid man. He must have bribed the chimney-sweep boy to put it there! How I *hate* him.'

'I'm sorry. I'm really, really sorry,' said Jessica. 'I wish I could help you.'

'*You?* Help me? The only way you can help me, my girl, is by jumping off that plank and letting me have Apple Manor.'

'What will you do when Father gets back? You won't be able to kill him.'

'Oh, won't I? I shall kill him, *Special Child*, after he has installed the new figurehead. If he fails, then Apple Manor will die; but at least no one else will have it. Now jump off that plank before I push you off.'

'Haven't you forgotten something?' Jessica held out Captain Pottage's things. She held them out wide, as if she was going to drop them in the moat. 'If I go, so do these. Then you'll never find them; the moat's bottomless.' Jessica opened the portrait of Captain Silas and Euphemia Pottage. At the sight of his picture, Miss Darknight's face crumpled in pain. Tears poured down her face and soaked into her blouse. She climbed on to the balcony. Jessica watched with a flash of fear as the woman stepped on to the end of the plank. She edged backwards, certain now that she was only seconds away from death.

'Give me his picture. Give it to me. All I want now is . . .' Miss Darknight stopped and lifted her head, as if to listen. The tears fell from her eyes still.

And then Jessica heard it too: a voice, so faint at

first that she thought she had imagined it. Then it came again, stronger this time.

'Father!' She peered down into the blizzard. 'Father!'

'Jessica! Jessica, what are you doing up there?'

It *was* her father; she'd know his tweed cloak and scruffy hat anywhere, even in a blizzard!

'It's that horrible man! It's that useless, good-for-nothing carpenter! How dare he come back, just when I've got everything organised? Give me my husband back, Jessica Sweetapple.'

'Get off there this minute, Jessica! I'm coming up to get you!' Mr Sweetapple hurried towards the house, his head bent against the blizzard.

Jessica's heart sang. Her father had returned. She shifted along the plank to get back on to the balcony, but Miss Darknight was blocking her way. She reached for the portrait in Jessica's hand.

'Into the moat with you! You'll not ruin my plans, Miss Sharp-Tongue Sweetapple.' Miss Darknight stepped quickly towards her and in that moment Jessica felt a great sadness. She was about to die.

Her mother leaned across the balcony, arms outstretched towards her. 'Jessica!' There was such pain in her voice that Jessica felt it like a knife in her own chest.

Mrs Sweetapple grabbed at Miss Darknight's skirt but the woman pulled it away before she could get hold. 'Leave her alone! Let her get down! Think what you're doing. Please!'

The tears still coursed down Euphemia Darknight's face. She couldn't see clearly. She stumbled nearer and groped for the locket. For a second she loomed above Jessica like a fast, black crow.

The plank bent so much that it was an almost vertical line pointing towards the moat. Jessica saw Lilith's frightened face peering down at them both. She held on with all her strength. She tried to blot out Miss Darknight's screams as the woman lost her footing; and in the same moment it appeared to her as if Miss Darknight was a blur and a bundle of black arms and legs. She seemed to hover in the air for a moment before falling and falling, down to the deep, dark depths of the moat, her screams growing fainter as she fell. But then Lilith followed too. It looked almost as though something had yanked her from the balcony. She followed with her arms outstretched like a bird, and Jessica saw that she was attached to Miss Darknight by a long silver thread. Just a brief second before they hit the ice, Lilith and Miss Darknight became one. Lilith's body merged with the woman's as if they were Russian dolls.

Jessica sat for a time, numbed with shock. It was only the sight of her father's reaching arms that gave her the strength to edge back to the balcony and into the safety of her very own bedroom.

17. The restoration of Apple Manor

A roll of parchment hung from Sir Lancelot's leaf on the Family Tree. It was addressed to Jessica and jiggled erratically as she reached to untie the strip of cloth which held it there.

Well done, Special Child. Euphemia and Lilith Darknight are now on the ship, and word has come that Captain Pottage intends to join them soon. We

very much hope that they will learn to take their place
with us. You may also be interested to learn that
Granny Harriet has peacefully entered the Great Sleep.
Now your task is almost done and Lady Imogen joins
me in sending love and best wishes for the final
outcome: the restoration of Apple Manor.

> *Your loving Ancestor,*
> *Sir Lancelot Sweetapple*

Jessica read the message and smiled to know that Sir Lancelot was so pleased with her. But no one was celebrating. Her father had failed in his task, and although he had searched the greatest forests on earth he had not found the right wood for the figurehead. And until he did, Apple Manor could not be restored.

Even so, it was wonderful to be all together again. Jessica stood between her parents, enjoying the feeling of their arms round her. Her mother was completely solid now that her father had returned; she was all warm flesh, as soft and sweet as a tea-time scone. Jessica leaned against her, breathed in the smell of her. It was a secure place from which to gaze at the ravages of the great house. Things had stopped getting worse since Miss Darknight had returned to the ship, but they certainly weren't getting any better.

She gazed at the poor old Family Tree, its limp branches drooping across the tiles of the hallway, the wood soft and bendy. In the centre was an enormous branch she hadn't noticed before. It looked firmer than the others and not so dark. She wriggled out of her parents' arms to take a closer look.

She hated the feel of the branches as she pushed them aside; they draped across her shoulders and stuck to her hair. She had loved this tree once but she couldn't love it now. It seemed as though its dying, sticky droopiness wanted to capture her, as if it were a spider and she a fly in the cobweb of its branches.

When she put her hand on the branch she had been working towards, she found that it was firm and strong. She held on to it and put her cheek against its beautiful rough bark. The crystal apple sent pulses of light through the entire tree; it danced between its branches and wove magical skeins of colour round its leaves. Jessica knew that in this branch lay the future of Apple Manor.

She pushed the sticky branches aside, hardly feeling them in her eagerness to speak. 'It's here! Father, this is the wood for the figurehead! I've found it! It was here all the time!'

Richard Sweetapple locked himself away in his workshop and would not come out, except to eat. Jessica and Mrs Sweetapple both longed to ask him how the figurehead was coming on, but he wouldn't speak of it. His eyes had a faraway look and they both knew that he was locked in some sort of struggle with the wood; he was striving to find the figure inside.

Jessica and her mother went for long walks in the snow. They walked past the schoolroom and looked for the wooden children. But they had gone. It was a relief not to hear their wooden laughter. Jessica longed for the time when her friends would return. The silence in the village waited for them. When would they come back?

It was a silence almost complete, except for the sounds which came from Richard Sweetapple's workshop as he coaxed and persuaded the wood to match the vision in his head. Each day wound slowly round, biding its time, waiting for the figurehead to come, until one day Jessica's father entered the great hall with a smile on his face. He stepped carefully across the uneven tiles and made his way to the kitchen where he stood in the doorway. There was no need for words.

They hurried through the snow to the workshop. It was warm inside and smelled of sweet dust and wood shavings. Mr Sweetapple shut the door quietly, then lifted a cloth from the enormous shape on the workbench. Jessica gasped.

For she was looking at two figureheads, not one. They grew, waist upwards, from a great wooden apple. Their arms twined round each other, and Lady Imogen smiled down at her distant granddaughter:

Jessica Sweetapple, the Special Child of the Generations.

Jessica and her mother mopped up the sap which had dripped on to her bedroom floor and then they retreated and listened, their ears to the door, as Mr Sweetapple hammered and planed and glued. They were not allowed in until he had finished.

They knew when that moment had come because the house gave a great, shuddering sigh. It began to breathe again, the gentle purr of contentment it had made ever since the house was built, and which only a Sweetapple could hear. Every now and then, an outsider would hear it too. Jessica's mother had heard it as she passed by on a solitary walk one day. Richard Sweetapple had married her at once, before she could reach the end of the village and forget the things she had always known about life and death.

Now she pushed open the door to her daughter's bedroom. They lifted their heads to look at the figurehead, soaring proudly against the enormously high ceiling.

After a long, breathless time, Jessica glanced out of her bedroom window. The tears had gone.

A sharp crack made them glance at the walls. They saw them shiver and straighten and then let out great sighs of relief.

They stepped out on to the landing and looked down into the hallway. The marble tiles were settling down and straightening themselves, the walls creaked and cracked to stand tall and straight again. Through the stained glass windows a faint beam of sunlight penetrated. The Family Tree lifted its branches. Blossom began to sprout as buds unfurled. Snow dripped steadily from the windowledges and slid from the roof. The bells from the church tower pealed joyfully.

And then all at once a knocking came at the door. Jessica Sweetapple ran down the stairs and across the hall. She dragged open the great front door to find her lost friends standing there.

Mrs Sweetapple followed, holding out her daughter's coat. 'Don't be back late,' she said. 'Put on your boots!'

'I won't!' she called. 'I will.' And she skipped down the path with Oliver, Thomas and Guy, Kathryn, Sally and Coralie, Lauren, Joel and Alastair, Tony and Jonathan, Janet, Michael and Edward. All her very best friends. They ran down the lane towards adventure. And Jessica Sweetapple ran with them.